I0534989

RANSOM FOR LOVE
A Collection Of Three Plays

'Dipo Toby Alakija

ISBN: 978-49874-8-1
ISBN: 978-978-4987-4-8-6

First Published In 2012.
Printed in the United States

Republished In 2016 By
The Publishing House Of

CALVARY ROCK RESOURCES

19, Ajina Street, Ikenne Remo,
Ogun State,
Nigeria.

36, Thomson road
Gorton
Manchester
M18 7QQ
United Kingdom

270 Madison Avenue
Suite 1500, New York, NY 10016
United States

www.calvaryrock.org

PLAY ONE

A CRACK IN THE HOME

A CRACK IN THE HOME

What else can be more dangerous
Like a crack in the home?
What else can be more deadly
Like a house on fire?

Where else is the root of all crimes
Except from a divided home?
What are the products of divorce
Except lawless children?

The foundations of all families
Are the foundations of all nations
The problems of every nation
Begin with marital discord

The unity and love in a family
Promotes unity and love in the nation
The insecurity in any family
Is a threat to the security of the nation

ACT ONE SCENE ONE

(Kola and Mercy sit at the dining table, facing each other. Sade is in her school uniform eating with them.)

KOLA: *(tastes part of the stew. He frowns.)* I'm not sure I like the taste of your stew.

MERCY: *(looks at Sade who looks impatiently at both of them.)* Must you criticize me right in the presence of the child?

KOLA: The child must learn from all sorts of things I've been trying to tolerate about you.

MERCY: Do you really feel you are in the position to judge any of my actions? Has it ever occurred to you that you're becoming more and more provocative?

KOLA: Now shut up your big mouth before I deal ruthlessly with you!

MERCY: You can call me names if you like but you too must learn never to hang out your long tongue when talking to me.

KOLA: *(stands up in anger.)* Are you talking to me?

MERCY: *(looks steadily at him.)* Yes, I am. I suppose you want to beat me up.

KOLA: You think I cannot beat sense into you?

MERCY: Who is holding you back?

KOLA: *(goes to her. She stands up to face him boldly.)* You are ready to strike back, aren't you?

MERCY: You dare touch me… I'll prove it to you that it's not only dog that can bit so hard.

KOLA: Then I'll be glad to break your jaw first… *(He moves forward.)*

SADE: Dad, mum!

KOLA: You go to your room now! *(Sade hesitates.)* Go now!

SADE: I'll kill myself if anything happens to either of you! I promise you! *(She hurries to her room, crying all the way.)*

MERCY: *(looks at her as she goes away. She glares at Kola.)* The child is gone now. Go ahead and suit yourself.

KOLA: One of these days, you are going to push me to the wall. That time, I will give you what you really deserve. *(He picks his brief case and leaves the room. Mercy goes inside the room).*

ACT ONE SCENE TWO

(Sade is on the bed with her face on the pillow, crying. The door is knocked. Mercy comes inside the room.)

MERCY: You will miss the school bus if you don't start going now.

SADE: *(sobs.)* I'm not going to school.

3

MERCY: Why?

SADE: *(sits up on the bed)*. You're asking me why, mum? I've been trying to understand many things but I'm yet to understand why you and dad are constantly at each other's necks.

MERCY: You don't use a language like that to speak about us. We are still your parents, no matter what happens.

SADE: *(looks at her.)* Mum, with due apology, I don't think I'm in the mood for any lesson about how to address you and dad. As I can see, the lesson you've been trying to teach me does not apply to both of you. How could you be teaching me one thing and be doing another thing?

MERCY: Okay, I'm sorry if it seems as if we are not leading you by example. You know things were not like this before now. I'm sure everything will soon be fine.

SADE: The first time you said everything will soon be fine, I believed you. Now I don't because I've lost count of the times you told me everything will be fine. Nothing is fine - nothing will ever be fine, mum! *(She begins to cry again.)*

MERCY: *(goes to sit beside her.)* It's okay, child. I guess I have to confess that things are not the same between me and your father. He seems to have changed. I … don't know …. *(She looks sad.)* People are telling me that your father is going out with another woman and he's looking for reasons - any reason to divorce me.

SADE: *(looks her.)* What?

MERCY: I'm sorry I have to tell you this. I tried all I could to hide it from you but *(She looks withdrawn)* …. I don't know.

SADE: Mum, you …. you are not going to allow daddy to … to divorce you are you?

MERCY: With the way he is doing now, he may succeed getting a divorce from me.

SADE: Oh no! *(She bursts out into hysterical sobs. Mercy holds her shoulders, looking as if she will cry too).* What's going to happen to me?

MERCY: You will be fine…

ACT ONE SCENE THREE

(The students are seated in the classroom in the school with Miss James, standing and addressing the class. Sade later comes into the class room. Miss James pauses and stares at her.)

SADE: *(bows.)* Good Morning, ma.

4

MISS JAMES: Good Morning. Why are you just coming?

SADE: I ... I missed the school bus, ma.

MISS JAMES: And why did you miss the school bus?

SADE: *(looks at other students who are all staring at her).* My... parents ...they ...are... *(She looks as if she would cry.)*

MISS JAMES: *(goes to pat her on shoulder.)* It's okay, my dear. You'll tell me about it later. *(She gestures her to take her seat before she looks at the rest. Sade mumbles her thanks and goes to take her seat.)* We were talking about the problem of industrialization. Sumbo said one of them is lack of good transportation. Is she correct?

CLASS: Yes, ma.

MISS JAMES: Yes, she is right. Can anyone tell me another problem that is associated with industrialization? *(One of the students raise up her hand).* Yes, tell us...

ACT ONE SCENE FOUR

(It is in the staff room during the recess. Miss James calls one of the students called, Segun)

MISS JAMES: Young man, are you in JS 3 class?

SEGUN: Yes, ma.

MISS JAMES: You know Sade Olufemi?'

SEGUN: Yes, ma.

MISS JAMES: You go and tell her to meet me in the hall right now.

SEGUN: Yes, ma. *(The student hurries away).*

MISS JAMES: *(puts her things in the drawer. She looks at Miss Kayode, sitting by her table).* I'm going to the hall.

MISS KAYODE: What's happening in the hall?

MISS JAMES: I want to counsel one of the students. She seemed troubled. I want to find out what's wrong with her.

MISS KAYODE: I see. *(Miss James goes out of the staff room).*

ACT ONE SCENE FIVE

(Sade lays her head on the table while everybody plays in the class. Jully goes to her with some drinks and fish rolls. She taps her gently on the shoulder).

JULLY: Sade, I brought you some snacks. *(She draws a chair and sits beside her)* Come on, Sade, eat something. *(Sade raise up her head, drying her tears).* Whatever is happening, I'm sure it's not as serious as losing someone you love so much.

SADE: I'm about to lose the people who are so dear to me.

JULLY: *(frowns)* Who?

SADE: My parents.

JULLY: What? Are they sick or something?

SADE: No, they are not sick.

JULLY: What makes you think you're about to lose them?

SADE: I can't tell you that. I'm ashamed of it.

JULLY: It's okay if you don't want to talk about it. *(She gives her the fish rolls. She shakes her head).*

SADE: I don't feel like taking anything. *(Just then Segun comes into the class).*

SEGUN: Hay, Sade. Miss James wants you to meet her in the hall.

SADE: Okay. *(She stands up to go)* I'll see you later.

JULLY: *(shows her the drinks and the fish rolls.)* Do you want me to keep these for you?

SADE: *(Shakes her head.)* No, thanks. *(Then she goes away).*

ACT TWO SCENE ONE

(Miss James enters the hall where the students are engaged in one activity or the other. She goes to sit on the bench. One of the students, Toyin goes to greet her.)

TOYIN: Good afternoon, ma.

MISS JAMES: Good afternoon. How are you today?

TOYIN: I'm fine. Thank you, ma.

MISS JAMES: Did you do the assignment Miss Kayode gave you last week?

TOYIN: Yes, ma.

MISS JAMES: Good. You continue to do your best in your academics and, before you know it, you are already a doctor. Is that not what you plan to become?

TOYIN: Yes, I'll like to be a doctor.

MISS JAMES: If you really want to be a doctor, you must improve on your science subjects. You understand?

TOYIN: Yes, ma.

MISS JAMES: If you have problem with any subject, you can see Miss Kayode. I'm sure she'll do all she can to help you. *(Sade comes to join them in the hall). Hey, Sade. (She makes space for her to sit).* Come and sit down here. *(Sade goes to sit beside her.)* Toyin, you can go. We'll see later. *(Toyin goes away. Miss James looks at Sade.)* I can see that you were very troubled this morning. Can you tell me the problem?

SADE: *(looks reluctant for a moment.)* My parents are not in good terms. They are always … em… arguing….

MISS JAMES: You don't have to let that border you. Argument is normal in everyday activities.

SADE: *(There is brief silence.)* I … em… I don't know how to explain this. Their argument is not the normal thing. They almost fought each other this morning.

MISS JAMES: *(pats her on the shoulder.)* Still, there is nothing you should be bordered about.

SADE: My … mother told me she may divorce my father …

MISS JAMES: *(frowns)* why?

SADE: I … don't know.

MISS JAMES: *(looks thoughtful.)* In that case, you really have to tell them what you feel about it. Do they go to Church?

SADE: Not all the time. But we are Christians.

MISS JAMES: Christians don't divorce. There is nowhere in the Bible that encourages divorce. *(She looks thoughtful again)*If someone like the pastor in your Church talks to them about the mind of God about it, they may change their mind.

SADE: I don't know if they will listen to anyone. I'm so confused.

MISS JAMES: *(moves closer to her.)* You really have to do something about it. It's not good for couples to get divorced. It always affects the children. So you must do all you can to keep your parents together.

SADE: I …. I don't know what to do. *(She looks as if she would cry.)* Miss James, can you please talk to my mother about this?

MISS JAMES: No, I …. can't. It's not my business.

SADE: I am your business, Miss James. *(She kneels down.)* Please, Miss James, do it for me. *(There is another silence.)*

MISS JAMES: *(sighs.)* Okay, I'll talk to her.

SADE: Can we go together today?

MISS JAMES: Oh no …..

SADE: Please…

MISS JAMES: *(After a moment.)* Okay.

SADE: Thank you, ma.

ACT TWO SCENE TWO

(On the assembly ground, the students are dismissed. The boarding house students go to their hostels while the day students go towards the bus. Miss James, Jully and Sade go to the bus).

JULLY: When are you coming back from the town?

7

MISS JAMES: Soon as I complete what I'm going there to do *(She sits beside the driver while Sade and other students sit behind them. The bus soon drives away).*

ACT TWO SCENE THREE

(Mercy sits on the couch in the sitting room, looking thoughtful. She occasionally shakes her head thoughtfully. A moment later, the door is knocked).

MERCY: You can come in. The door is not locked. *(Sade and Miss James come into the sitting room. Mercy smiles at them.)*

MISS JAMES: Good afternoon, ma.

MERCY: Good afternoon. You're welcome. *(Sade goes to kneel down in front of her).*

SADE: Good afternoon, mum.

MERCY: How are you, my dear?

SADE: *(stands up. She gestures at Miss James)* This is my school teacher, Miss James.

MERCY: Oh, how are you?

MISS JAMES: I'm fine. Thank you, ma.

MERCY: *(stands up.)* Please, sit down.

MISS JAMES: *(sits down.)* Thank you, ma.

MERCY: What can I offer you?

MISS JAMES: Nothing, ma. I just come to see you for a little problem.

MERCY: All the same, let's get you some cold drinks. *(She looks at Sade)*. Come on, get her some cold minerals in the fridge.

MISS JAMES: Thank you, ma. *(Sade goes away).*

MERCY: *(sits down again)* I hope the problem has nothing to do with my daughter.

MISS JAMES: Actually, it has to do with her and the family.

MERCY: I see *(She looks thoughtful. Sade brings the minerals on a tray and set it in front of Miss James. She opens the minerals and goes to sit down).*

MISS JAMES: Sade, I don't want you around for now, please.

SADE: Okay, ma. *(She goes to her room)*

MISS JAMES: The discussion may upset her.

MERCY: I see.

MISS JAMES: *(takes some of the drinks).* Sade is one of my favorites students in the class. She's a very sensitive girl if you don't mind my choice of words. *(She pauses for a while before she continues)* This morning, she came late to the school. I asked her to meet me during the recess. She told me of the

8

problem in the family.

MERCY: *(looks thoughtful)* I see.

MISS JAMES: There's no argument about the fact that there's a problem which can affect her in the school. Actually, I wouldn't have come to intrude into what looks like a family affair if she had not begged me to talk to you.

MERCY: What did she say the problem is?

MISS JAMES: She said you're planning to divorce her father. *(There is silence)* I'm sorry if I'm going too far.

MERCY: Oh, no, you're not. In fact, you really impress me by coming here to talk to me about it.

MISS JAMES: *(sighs)* That's a relief.

MERCY: *(smiles)* You expect me to react negatively to that?

MISS JAMES: Yes. Not everybody likes people coming to them to discuss their family issues.

MERCY: What do you want to say about the problem?

MISS JAMES: I want you to have a second thought about the divorce. It's going to devastate Sade Besides, children are the ones that suffer most whenever their parents divorce. I've had the opportunities to counsel children of divorced parents. What's common about them is the foundation of their lives that characterized with anger, confusion, frustration and even depression. Many of them end up being frustrated at the early stage of their lives. So, please, madam, I want you to have a second thought about the issue; at least for the sake of the child.

MERCY: Em......Mrs...

MISS JAMES: I'm Miss James, ma.

MERCY: I see... Em... did Sade tell you I'm the one planning to divorce her father?

MISS JAMES: Actually, I don't know who is behind the idea but I know it takes both husband and wife to agree before they can divorce.

MERCY: It's not my fault really. My husband is becoming more and more irresponsible. He almost beat me up this morning right in front of the poor girl. Imagine a situation like that. He criticizes and insults me right in her presence. I know the girl has every reason to be so upset, but it's never my fault. I tried my best to make peace with him but he is looking for any reason to kick me out of the house and then justify himself before his family and mine. Obviously, when a man begins to behave like that, he is finding ways to replace his wife.

MISS JAMES: You have no reason to conclude that he wants to

9

replace you, do you?

MERCY: Fortunately, I do. Many people who always see him with another woman confirmed that he is having extra marital affairs.

MISS JAMES: That does not give you the cause to divorce him.

MERCY: Why not?

MISS JAMES: You have Sade to put into consideration. Besides, your marriage as far as Africans are concerned is a weapon to check his excesses, at least in the presence of his family.

MERCY: He doesn't see it that way. He sees my marriage with him as a chain which he feels he must break at all cost. That is the reason he is behaving like this. He feels if he makes life miserable for me, I would be too willing to give him a divorce. Fortunately or unfortunately, he is making a progress in making me feel so miserable that I'm considering giving it to him before he asks for it.

MISS JAMES: I believe you can still hang on until God intervenes. You don't have to give him the chance to divorce you. Divorce is a monster that can destroy many other things apart from home.

MERCY: You don't understand what I'm going through. The reason you cannot get the picture of how it feels to face a problem like this is because you're not married.

MISS JAMES: My parents are married and they are still married even though they are getting old.

MERCY: Your mother is fortunate to have your father. I'm not.

MISS JAMES: It's not a matter of luck. Perhaps if I tell what happened when I was in primary school, you'll understand what I mean. *(She looks thoughtful as she relates the incident in flashbacks which follow in sequence. The flash back moves from one to another as she relates the incident)* My parents started having some quarrels about every little thing in the house to the extent that my father constantly ordered my mother out of the house. My mother refused to leave.

ACT TWO SCENE FOUR
(Flashback)

(Mr James takes Mrs James bags from the room. He goes in the second time and brings another bag. This time Mrs James follows him and takes the bag back into the room.)

MR. JAMES: You must go back to your family today and learn how to behave! *(As Mrs James takes the second bag, Mr James pushes her on the couch. Mrs James takes the bag again.*

He snatches it from her) You must get back to your people today before there can be peace in this house.

MRS. JAMES: You and your people would have to take me back!

MR. JAMES: You this woman, you are looking for trouble. *(He grabs the bag from her. They begin to struggle until a child comes in.)*

CHILD: *(In childlike manner.)* Why are you fighting, Mummy, Daddy? *(The couple stops struggling.)*

MRS. JAMES: Your father wants to drive me away from the house. He doesn't want me to take care of you?

CHILD: Why?

MR. JAMES: *(goes to lift the child up.)* Don't mind your mother. *(He looks at Mrs James who makes face at him. He enters the room.)*

ACT TWO SCENE THREE B

MISS JAMES: My mother got so tired of the marriage that she went to her uncle who stood as her father during her wedding. She complained that my father find every reason to divorce him. She told her uncle that she wanted to divorce her. She asked him the best way she could do that. My great uncle who seemed to understand the problem advised her....

ACT TWO SCENE FIVE
(Flashback)

(Mrs James and Papa sits outside the house, talking)

PAPA: You really want to know the best way to handle the issue of divorce?

MRS JAMES: Yes, Uncle. I'll do anything to hurt him before I give him the divorce.

PAPA: When you get home, do all you can to please him. You can prepare him the food he likes most. When he wakes up in the morning, kneel to greet him. Kiss him if he gives you the chance. After pleasing him for three months, you can then divorce him. That will really hurt him.

MRS JAMES: That's a brilliant idea. I'm going to do just that.

ACT TWO SCENE THREE C

MISS JAMES: She did all she could to please my father. Within a short time, my father began to fall in love with my mother afresh. He

11

bought her presents every time. Before anyone knew it, both of them were in love again as if they just met. One day, my mother visited her uncle. He did not hesitate to ask if she has divorced my father. She asked him why she should divorce him. After all, both of them were in love.My great uncle laughed at her. He knew all along the real problem that was threatening the marriage was patience and tolerance.

You see madam, we all have our faults. If only we'll pretend not to see the faults of our neighbor and focus on how to address our own faults, we'll be able to tolerate each other. If one keeps looking at other people's faults without seeing his, he'll try to justify all his acts both wrong and right ones. But the truth is: the fault is ours. Let's allow our friends, neighbors and whoever to treat us like a fool as we love them. Then we'll see that there's nothing as powerful as love. If you love your husband despite all he's doing to you, he'll change one day.

Besides all the reasons I have given you, God hates divorce. If you do what God hates, you are not likely to find favor before him. I know it's hard to keep hanging on, especially when you have every reason to put an end to the marriage but I tell you you will win God's approval and the respect of many people, including your daughter. You see, nothing matters more to the girl like seeing the two of you together. You will devastate her if you are separated.

MERCY: *(looks thoughtful for a while before she sighs)* You have made so many valid points. I'll try to do as you advised.

MISS JAMES: Thank you very much for that decision. *(She stands up)*I must start going now.

MERCY: *(stands up as well)* Thanks so much for taking the time and pain to talk to me about my family. I really appreciate it. *(She looks towards the room)* Sade! *(Sade comes out.)* Come and see your teacher off to the garage. *(Miss James is the first to go out of the house. Mercy gives Sade some money)* Make sure you pay for her transportation.

ACT TWO SCENE SIX

(Sade and Miss James walk down the street, talking.)

MISS JAMES: Your mother promised to do all she can to keep the marriage. You don't have to worry about a thing. You just try to be a very good girl. Be close to your father. Try and talk to him about how you feel if he divorces your mother. Who can tell if that will help him to see things in another way that is different from his?

SADE: Thank you very much, ma. You're very kind.

MISS JAMES: *(smiles at her)* Thank you for the complement. *(A motor bike stops when she waves at him.)* Would you take me to O and A Academy, please?

OKADA MAN: Can you pay two hundred naira?

MISS JAMES: I'll give you one hundred Naira.

OKADA MAN: The place is far, you know.

MISS JAMES: I'll give you one hundred naira. Nothing more, nothing less.

OKADA MAN: Okay. *(Miss James sits behind him . Sade quickly goes to give the Okada man the money.)* Madam, the young lady has paid me the money.

MISS JAMES: What? Please return the money.

SADE: Please, Miss James. My mother insists that we pay for your transport

MISS JAMES: Okay. Thanks. See you tomorrow. *(The motorbike drives away.)*

ACT TWO SCENE SEVEN

(Kola comes inside the sitting room, Sade reads in the sitting room while Mercy lies on the couch. Mercy stands up to meet him with smiles)

SADE: *(looks at him)* Welcome, daddy. *(Mercy attempts to help Kola takes his bag but he brushes her aside).*

KOLA: *(goes past Sade to his room)* Hello, Sade. *(Mercy goes to sit down, looking unhappy. Sade looks at Mercy and goes to sit down beside her)*

SADE: You can't give up trying to please him, mum.

MERCY: I don't know why I have to do all these.

SADE: You're doing it because of me.

MERCY: *(In a whisper)* Alright, I'll do it because of you.

ACT THREE SCENE ONE

(Kola is in the office, going through some papers. The Office Assistance (O.F) knocks the door and comes inside)

O.F: Miss Bimbo Fame is asking of you, Sir.

KOLA: Send her in. *(He continues to look through the papers when Bimbo is ushered inside the office. He looks at her and brightens up as O.F leaves the office, closing the door behind him.)* Hello, Bimbo.

BIMBO: You are not surprised I come here?

KOLA: Why should I?

BIMBO: I've been expecting your call since yesterday. Since you didn't call, I feel I should come to see you.

KOLA: I'm sorry. I was busy all through yesterday. Since you have come here, we might as well go to my house and have some fun. How about that?

BIMBO: How about your wife?

BIMBO: She'll be at work now. Even if she is around, I still own the house. I can as well bring in anybody I like.

BIMBO: You know I'm a peace-loving woman. I don't want problem from anyone. I'm ready to play hide and seek game as long as it is for the sake of peace.

KOLA: *(laughs)* Look at yourself talking about peace.

BIMBO: Am I not peace loving?

KOLA: If you are really looking for peace, why should we play this game at all?

BIMBO: You know I can't help loving you. If not for love, I wouldn't be going out with you in the first place, let alone thinking of getting married to you. Although I never ask you of the chances of getting married to you, I can't help thinking of it. May be I should ask of the chance.

KOLA: For now, the chance is a bit remote. For one, I've got no one in my family that supports the idea of putting my wife away. Everybody, especially my mother seems to love my wife. So no matter what I complain about her, no one would listen. Secondly, my daughter who means so much to me is threatening to to harm herself because of the constant misunderstanding. I was expecting the quarrel to lead to separation but I don't know when that is going to be. I just want a situation that will justify whatever action I take about her.

BIMBO: So where is this jumping around with you going to lead us to?

KOLA: It depends on the situation.

BIMBO: What situation? You are an African, aren't you? So you have the privilege to marry as many wives as you want.

KOLA: You realize our marriage is statutory.

BIMBO: So what?

KOLA: So I can have only one wife.

BIMBO: If you have more than one wife, you will be taken to jail?

KOLA: That's what the law says.

BIMBO: And who will take you to jail?

KOLA: *(stands up as he arranges the papers)* You are becoming a pest. Let's go and have some fun before we run out of time.

BIMBO: *(stands on her feet too)* We really have to talk about this. I've got to know if I'm wasting my time with you.

KOLA: *(looks at her face)* You are not wasting your time with me. I can assure you that. I just let you know how far we still have to go before the issue of marriage can come in. *(He puts on his suit and waves to the door)* Shall we go now and make the best out of the time we have left? *(They leave the office)*

ACT THREE SCENE TWO

(Sade and Jully are at the café, sitting and eating snacks.)

JULLY: I suppose things are getting better back at home?

SADE: No. My father is not responding to my mother's nice treatment. I'm beginning to think my father has made up his mind about my mother.

JULLY: What do you mean?

SADE: I don't really want to talk about it.

JULLY: *(pats her on the shoulder.)* It's okay. *(She sips her drinks.)* I'm sure everything will soon be okay.

SADE: I hope so. I'm praying seriously that God should intervene in this. I know it is the devil who wants to break my family. My father is not as hard to please as he seems now. I mean he's such a gentleman. There was a time I day dreamt of a man like that to be my husband when I'm old enough to get married.

JULLY: You are right to think it is the devil. My elder sister has that problem.

SADE: *(looks interested)* Really? *(Jully nods)* How did she resolve the problem?

JULLY: I've been trying to tell you that the problem is common everywhere in Nigeria, America, Europe - everywhere. When problems like that occur, the best thing to do is to hand everything over to God in prayer. My sister was fortunate enough to have a brother-in-law who is a pastor. So they prayed and prayed until her husband came to realise that he was going to hell by having another woman apart from his wife.

SADE: You will have to join me in praying about it, wont you?

JULLY: I was thinking of how we can fast and pray together about it.

SADE: When can we do that?

JULLY: Let's make it next week.

SADE: Thank you so much. You are really a friend indeed and in need.

ACT THREE SCENE THREE

(Kola and Bimbo enter the sitting room. She goes to sit down while he goes to get her some drinks.)

BIMBO: *(looks at Kola as he brings the drinks.)* You are more comfortable here than the last time I came here.

KOLA : *(gives her the drink.)* Well, for now, this is the best I get for myself.

BIMBO: Kola, I need to ask of the plan you have for me. What is this relationship going to get us to?

KOLA: I wish you don't bring that up again.

BIMBO: By that, I can get the impression that you are just using me.

KOLA: Of course not!

BIMBO: Then let's define the relationship right now.

KOLA: Oh ,Come on baby. This is not the time for that. Let's check out the bedroom.

BIMBO: No. Not until the time you tell me what you want to make out of me.

KOLA: If I say I know it now, that will be a lie. Don't let me lie to you by telling you anything. I can only assure you that I love you.

BIMBO: Really? *(He smiles at her and nods)*

KOLA: Let me prove it to you in the bedroom. *(She stands up and follows him inside the bedroom.)*

ACT THREE SCENE FOUR

(Mercy opens the door to the sitting room, looking puzzle. She looks round the room.)

MERCY: Darling, are you at home? *(Just then Kola and Bimbo comes out of the room)* what?! *(Mercy rushes to grip Bimbo. She quickly moves sideways. Kola steps between them.)*

KOLA: If you dare touch her, you will be dead before you know it. *(He looks at Bimbo)* Let's go, sweetheart. *(They leave the sitting room. He calls out from outside)* Make sure you lock the door, kitchen wife! *(Mercy looks furious. She hesitates for a while before she rushes into the room and starts bringing out her things.)*

ACT THREE SCENE FIVE

(Sade, Jully and other students are having a group study in the class when Miss James comes in.)

MISS JAMES: Sade. *(Sade looks at her and stands up to go to her.*

) Let's go and talk. *(Sade looks nervous as they go outside)* It's not that bad. Your mother came here and informed me that she has packed out of the house.

SADE: What? I.....thought she agreed to do what you told her.

MISS JAMES: Yes, but.....em....according to her, she could not stand what she found out today.

SADE: What did she find out?

MISS JAMES: She said your father brought a lady into the house.

SADE: *(in a whisper)* I see...

MISS JAMES: She wants you to go to Mrs Smith's house. She said you know the place. She'll be waiting for you at the place.

SADE: For doing this to me, I'm neither going home nor seeing her. I'm staying right in school.

MISS JAMES: You're not a boarding house student, remember.

SADE: *(begins to cry.)* Miss James, if my parents let me down, you're not going to let me down, are you?

MISS JAMES: Sade, there's a limit we can go to help you.

SADE: *(goes on her kneels.)* Let me stay with you, please.

MISS JAMES: I can't do that.

SADE: *(stands up.)* I've promised my parents that if anything happens to either of them I'm going to kill myself. You cannot tell if dying is the solution to this problem

MISS JAMES: Christians don't talk like that. You are supposed to think of a way out, not to hurt yourself.

SADE: If no one is going to help me, what am I supposed to do except to do it? I'll go to where people will not see me. If I'm dead, it's better for me than to see my parents pulling themselves apart without putting me into consideration. *(She begins to walk quickly away. Miss James goes quickly after her.)*

MISS JAMES: Wait a minute, Sade. Let me think of what I can do. Meanwhile, I want you to realize that we're in the mess together - you and me.

SADE: Really? *(Miss James nods. She goes to hug her.)* I know I can always count on you.

ACT THREE SCENE SIX

(Miss James enters the principal's office while he looks through some papers).

PRINCIPAL: *(looks up.)* Oh, Miss James. I'm sorry I kept you waiting. I have to go through all these documents.*(He gestures her to sit. She sits down slowly).* You don't look yourself this afternoon. What seems to be the problem?

MISS JAMES: I'm concerned about one of the students, sir. Her parents are getting divorced.

PRINCIPAL: Divorce is the song we hear everyday all over the world.

MISS JAMES: But it's monster that upsets this girl so much that she is thinking of hurting herself.

PRINCIPAL: The best you can do to help the girl is to counsel her and help her get used to it.

MISS JAMES: The problem is more than that, sir. I wish I know how to explain this.

PRINCIPAL: What do you want us to do now?

MISS JAMES: I don't know. I thought you'll find a solution.

PRINCIPAL: If there's a problem you know you cannot handle, the best you can do is to avoid.

MISS JAMES: What if I cannot avoid it, sir?

PRINCIPAL: Pretend as if it's not there.

MISS JAMES: I can't, sir.

PRINCIPAL: Then that is the problem. You see, there would always be problems - both the ones you can solve and the one you can't. Your attitude towards it is what will determine if you're going to get a solution or not.

MISS JAMES: This girl said something which made me committed to her. She said if her parents let her down with the divorce, am I going to let her down.

PRINCIPAL: *(sighs after a brief silence)* Alright, I can see your point now. You can go and talk with her parents. If you can, persuade them to make her a boarding house student. If we have to give her a discount, we will; at least; for the sake of the girl. I can see that the girl looks up to us for help.

MISS JAMES: What if they don't take to the advice, what do I do?

PRINCIPAL: There's nothing else you can do. By the way, who registered the girl in the school?

MISS JAMES: I'm not sure who but I think it's her mother.

PRINCIPAL: Check her file and find that out. If it's her mother, try all you can to persuade her.

MISS JAMES: *(stands up.)* Okay. Thank you sir.

ACT FOUR SCENE ONE

(Miss James enter the staff room and goes to sit down. Miss kayode who is reading looks at her).

MISS KAYODE: Where have you been?

18

MISS JAMES: I went to see the principal.

MISS KAYODE: What for?

MISS JAMES: It's in connection with the student in my class.

MISS KAYODE: You mean Sade again?

MISS JAMES: I didn't know I told you about it. It's the same girl. (*She takes out some books to go through them*)

MISS KAYODE: Don't you think you are taking the case of the girl too personal?

MISS JAMES: (*opens one book after the other.*) I can't help it, not when the girl told me she will hurt herself if I try to pull out.

MISS KAYODE: Is it that serious?

MISS JAMES: I think it is. I just hope God will get me out of this soonest. (*Sade comes into the staff room*)

SADE: (*bows.*) Good afternoon, Miss kayode.

MISS KAYODE: Hay, sweetie. How are you?

SADE: I'm fine. Thank you, ma. (*She looks at Miss James*) You sent for me?

MISS JAMES: Oh yes. We are going to see your mother together.

SADE: Mrs James, I said…

MISS JAMES: You've got to trust me to handle this.

SADE: Okay, ma.

MISS JAMES: We see her after closing hour.

SADE: Okay, ma. (*She goes away.*)

ACT FOUR SCENE TWO

(*Mercy sits alone in Smith's room, looking thoughtful when the door bell rings. She jumps up to open the door*)

MISS JAMES: Good afternoon, ma.

MERCY: Good afternoon, Miss James. Where is my daughter?

MISS JAMES: She's outside.

MERCY: Why is she staying outside?

MISS JAMES: She is very upset. In fact, she wouldn't have come here if I did not come with her. We really have to talk before she could see you.

MERCY: (*sits down. She gestures her to the seat in front of her.*) Didn't you tell her why I have to pack out of the house?

MISS JAMES: Actually, I told her but she could not justify your action just as I did not.

MERCY: You can't say that! How would a woman feel if she finds a strange woman in her matrimonial home? As if that was not enough, he called me a kitchen wife in the presence of that

19

cheap prostitute. *(She bursts out crying. There is silence as she blows her nose with some tissue paper, drying her eyes.)* I could kill him and that woman in that mood but I didn't. I choose to leave the house for them. Now you and Sade are accusing pointing fingers at me. What would you do if you were in my shoe?

MISS JAMES: If I were in your shoe, I would hang on.

MERCY: Are you being honest?

MISS JAMES: Yes. If you see things in my way, you would not act like that. The situation is like someone using everything possible to get what is so precious to you. And you just gave that person the great chance to succeed. That precious thing is your marriage and the person who is trying to get it from you is not really that woman that is sharing your husband with you but the devil. If you see the whole thing this way, that will give you the strength to hang on. The problem is you kept seeing people doing all these harms to your marriage and you keep saying to yourself, "I just can't take it any more!" If there is any reason you should continue to endure, it is your daughter. By packing out, she felt you let her down.

MERCY: She can't feel that way. She knows what I've been through.

MISS JAMES: The other point you must get is that: she sees your marriage with her father as a legacy. You have to do all you can to ensure that you preserve it for her. If she gets married and a situation like this occurs, how would you advise her? Obviously, with the action you have taken so far, you can't advise her not to pack out of her matrimonial home, can you? *(Mercy looks thoughtful)* You see, madam, people don't go through so much for the fun of it but because they want to teach by examples. Unknown to you, Sade sees your marriage to her father as her dream - something she could be really proud of. Quite unfortunately, you shattered that dream by leaving her father. How do you expect her to feel? You know she is a sensitive teenage girl.

MERCY: What am I supposed to do now?

MISS JAMES: You have to go back home.

MERCY: I can't do that unless someone talks to her father first.

MISS JAMES: *(looks thoughtful)* If Sade and I go and appeal to him on your behalf, do you think he will listen.

MERCY: I can't guarantee that.

MISS JAMES: *(stands up.)* We'll try. I've promised Sade I'll do my best to help her.

MERCY: *(Standing as well)* Thank you very much. You're a very nice person.

MISS JAMES: Thank you. *(She leaves the room. She follows her.)*

ACT FOUR SCENE THREE

(Kola and Bimbo are coming from the room, talking.)

BIMBO: I wish I understand why I can't stay here overnight since your wife have packed out.

KOLA: I told you my daughter will be upset if she finds you here. It is bad enough for her to think that her mother has moved out of the house without seeing you here. I don't want her to jump into conclusion that I made her to pack out for you.

BIMBO: It doesn't make sense to me.

KOLA: Please, try and understand. *(He leads her to the door.)* We'll see tomorrow. *(As he opens the door, Sade and Miss James come to the house).*

MISS JAMES: Good afternoon, sir. *(She looks at Bimbo)* Good afternoon, ma. *(Sade looks down, murmurs her greetings and enters the sitting room).*

BIMBO: Good afternoon.

KOLA: Good afternoon. *(He looks at Bimbo)* We'll see later. *(He looks at Miss James)* Can I help you?

MISS JAMES: My name is Miss James. I'm Sade's teacher.

KOLA: I see. You're welcome. Please, come inside.

MISS JAMES: *(comes into the sitting room)* Thank you, sir. *(Sade is sitting on the couch, sobbing and using the back of her hand to dry her eyes).*

KOLA: *(goes to sit down)* What's wrong with you? (*He gestures at Miss James who is still standing to sit down).* Please, have your seat. *(Miss James sits opposite him)* I hope there's no problem, Miss James.

MISS JAMES: There is a little problem, sir. The problem seems upset Sade so much that I have to come and talk to you about it if you could grant me audience.

KOLA: What is the problem?

MISS JAMES: Her mother came to our school this afternoon and informed me that she's packed out of the house. She wanted Sade to meet her some where. Sade felt so upset that she wanted to hurt herself.

KOLA: Why would she hurt herself?

MISS JAMES: Actually, she's devastated by what looks like a crack in the marriage between you and her mother.

KOLA: *(in a harsh voice.)* What's the crack? Are you here to intrude into my family affairs?

MISS JAMES: Oh, no, sir. I mean well, sir. I'm here because Sade wanted me involved in this.

KOLA: Okay, thank you for coming. I can handle the matter myself. *(He stands up)* Can I see you off? *(Reluctantly, Miss James stands up. Sade begins to cry the more as Miss James left)*

MISS JAMES: I'll see you tomorrow, Sade. I'll try and talk to your mother.

KOLA: Lady, I appreciate what you're trying to do. But, please, stay out of this. It's none of your business. *(Miss James sighs helplessly and leaves. Sade stands up and hurries to her room, looking very upset.)*

ACT FOUR SCENE FOUR

(Mercy is still in Mrs Smith's sitting room, looking passive. A after a moment, the door is knocked. She quickly goes to open it. Miss James waits by the door)

MERCY: Please, come in, Miss James.

MISS JAMES: I don't have good news for you. I'm sorry. Your husband did not grant me audience.

MERCY: Actually, I expected it.

MISS JAMES: Well?

MERCY: He is a very difficult man.

MISS JAMES: If you ask me what I think, I'll say you gave him the chance to behave that way. He may have his short comings but you know it is not proper for a woman to pack out of her matrimonial home just like that.

MERCY: *(sighs.)* Okay, I accept the blame. What do we do about Sade? Can you persuade her to stay with me?

MISS JAMES: I left her there.

MERCY: But why?

MISS JAMES: I was practically ordered out of the house. *(Silence)* I'm sorry. I'll have to think of what else to do. I promise you I'll do something.

MERCY: Alright. Thank you very much.

MISS JAMES: Let me start going now. *(The two ladies go out of the room.)*

ACT FOUR SCENE FIVE

(Kola enters Sade's room slowly. Sade is sobbing on the bed).

KOLA: Sade … *(She is silent.)* Sade, I don't want you to think ill of me. I'm not the one that drove your mother away. So let's do all we can to get along with our lives.

SADE: *(sits up to look at him.)* You drove my mother away and I'm not going to forgive you for that.

KOLA: You're talking to me - your father!

SADE: *(looks angry.)* You're not the father I used to know. The father I know is a complete gentleman. He respects his family. He does not flirt around with ladies. *(Kola gives her a hard slap. She falls on her back and begins to cry).*

KOLA: Who is flirting around?

SADE: *(she sits up again.)* We met the lady you were planning to marry. My mother is right!

KOLA: She is right about what?

SADE: I don't have to say it. I've just realize that. You're the one tearing apart the family.

KOLA: So you are on your mother's side.

SADE: I'm not afraid to say yes!

KOLA: Do I own you any explanation?

SADE: No, daddy. You owe no one explanation except God because he gave my mother and me to you. We were once happy - so happy that I dreamt and prays always that God should give me the kind of father I have as a husband. *(She begins to cry again.)* But now, things have fallen apart because of another lady. I prayed and even fasted that God should do something but things continue to grow from bad to worse. I brought my school teacher to talk to you about it after she had talked to my mother but you sent her away. I don't know for how long I can bear all these pains and sorrow before I break down. I'm too young to face all these problem....*(She sobs more audibly.)*

KOLA: *(look sober.)* I'm sorry.

SADE: *(dries her tears.)* I have just one question to ask you. Why are you doing this to us? Are you tired of us?

KOLA: It's your mother.

SADE: You've been managing even before I was born. When did become too unmanageable for you. Did you see her with any man?

KOLA: You must realize that it's not only if she goes out with another man before she becomes unmanageable. By the way, who's been teaching you all these? Your school teacher or your mother?

SADE: Dad, I don't want you to consider me a kid because I'm not not any more. I saw things happening in this house and I have the brain to decode information because I'm not a dummy. *(Silence)* Dad, I want to say something I have never said before. The day I saw you and mummy singing and cooking meal together in the kitchen, I told myself I'll like to have a husband like you and I'll behave like mummy and we'll be happy together. Again, I had to change my mind when I saw you almost beat my mother. Have you asked yourself dad. What kind of legacy are you giving to me by breaking the family? How would you feel if I marry someone like you as I've been dreaming and he treats me the way you treat my mother? You'll be happy?*(Kola frowns, sighs and stands up slowly and silently. He goes out of the room, closing the door. Sade goes on her kneels and begins to pray silently and fervently)*

ACT FOUR SCENE SIX

(Kola sits on by the dinning table, taking his breakfast. Sade comes out of the room, ready to go to school).

SADE: Good morning, dad.

KOLA: *(cheerfully)* Good morning, my witty baby. *(She goes towards the door)* Aren't you taking your breakfast before you go?

SADE: I can manage.

KOLA: I woke up early to prepare this meal for the two us.

SADE: *(hesitates for a while before she goes to sit down).* Okay, I'll take some. *(She prays over the meal while he looks at her. Then she begins to eat. There is silence as they eat).*

KOLA: You may end up becoming a marriage counselor.

SADE: *(looks sharply at him.)* Why do you say that?

KOLA: What you said yesterday makes me think so. Tell me the truth. Who taught you all you said yesterday?

SADE: Dad ….

KOLA: Just tell me, please. It doesn't matter who. I'm only curious.

SADE: I pray that God should use me to speak to you.

KOLA: Do you really mean what you said about my marriage with your mother?

SADE: Yes, dad. I don't know which one you're referring to but I mean everything I said. If you and my mother stay together for life, it is a lasting for me and best legacy because it is the foundation of a good home. As the proverb says, charity begins at home.

KOLA: You talk like adult.

SADE: I learnt a lot of things from you and mum and my teachers and my friends in the school.

KOLA: *(sighs.)* If my marriage is giving you a legacy, would you give me another chance to make it work?

SADE: *(looks surprised)* Y- you mean it?

KOLA: Of course, yes. I want to give you the best of me. If keeping my marriage with your mother is the best, I will do it just for you.

SADE: What about the lady.

KOLA: I'll get rid of her.

SADE: Oh, dad, I'm so happy. *(She stands up to hug him)*

KOLA: You know where your mother is.

SADE: *(Nods)* Yes. She stays in Mrs smith house.

KOLA: We'll go and bring her home together today.

SADE: *(She gives a kiss on the check)* Oh, dad! You are the best father in the world and I'm so proud of you.

ACT FOUR SCENE SEVEN

(Miss James just finishes teaching in the classroom. Sade excitedly goes to her).

SADE: Miss James, you wont believe what happened if I tell you.

MISS JAMES: *(Curiously)* What happened?

SADE: My father wants me to take him to my mother. He wants to ask her to come home.

MISS JAMES: Oh, my good God. *(She holds her.)* Come and give me the full the full gist outside. *(They go out of the classroom.)*

ACT FOUR SCENE EIGHT

(Mercy walks round the room, looking passive. Then the door is knocked).

MERCY: Please, come in. *(Sade enters.)* Why do you take so long to come?

SADE: I have to get home first. I come with daddy.

MERCY: What?

KOLA: *(enters the room.)* We come together. We come to take you home, honey. *(Mercy looks surprised. She looks at Sade who is smiling).*

MERCY: Whatever has happened to you, I think it's one of the most wonderful things that has ever happened to me

KOLA: The credit goes to your daughter and her school teacher. They are of the opinion that one of the best things that can happen to a family is to stick together like glue. We'll start all over again and stick together, honey. What do you say?

MERCY: Let me get my things and we'll conclude it in our bedroom. *(She goes to another room.)*

SADE: *(Smiling at Kola)* I'm proud of you, dad.

KOLA: I'm more proud of you.

ACT FOUR SCENE NINE

(Kola and Bimbo are together in the office, talking.)

KOLA: I think I have to let you know what to make out of the relationship between us.

BIMBO: I've been waiting for it for so long.

KOLA: I don't think anything can come out of it.

BIMBO: *(looks agitated.)* What? I thought since your wife has moved out, we have a better chance of coming together.

KOLA: My wife and I have reconciled. In fact, so many events have over taken what I was thinking. I have decided to live a much more responsible life.

BIMBO: *(jumps on her feet.)* I should have seen it coming. You men are the same. *(She moves towards the door.)* I don't ever want to see you again. *(She goes out of the office and slams the door behind her.)*

PLAY TWO

RANSOM FOR LOVE

RANSOM FOR LOVE

The devil was her fiancé
They are to be married in hell
He had rights to her life
 For they will be married

Ransom for love
What price is it?
Ransom for heart
How much is it?

She met her real love
Walking into her wretched life
He was ready to pay the price
All because he loves her

Ransom for love...

She became so confused
That she never knew what to do
But she knew she would die
If she goes with the devil

Ransom for love....

Her real love got ready
To help her fight the war
Which she could not fight alone
In other to save herself

Ransom for love....

Her love paid the price
Without money without price
Through his sacrifice
All because he loves her

Ransom for love....

She never pays anything
To get her the salvation
Her real love paid everything
To get her the freedom

Ransom for love....

ACT ONE SCENE ONE

(Rosita and Augustine are in her living room, sitting opposite each other. She appears to be more interested in the magazine in her hand while Augustine stares at her, looking offended.)

AUGUSTINE: ... As a matter of fact, I can't stomach this ill treatment any longer.

ROSITA: *(still looks at the magazine.)* How do I maltreat you?

AUGUSTINE: I'm a man of dignity. So you don't expect me to fool around with any lady even though you know the number of ladies that will love to travel with me.

ROSITA: *(looks at him briefly with irritation.)* I wish you know how much you piss me off with your claims. Why not travel out with whoever you like and leave me alone? I told you I've got more than enough work to occupy me down here in Nigeria without you trying to force me to travel out and waste my time in Canada.

AUGUSTINE: You really consider the journey with me waste of time? What sort thing is that? *(There is silence as he goes to sit beside her on the couch.)* Can you tell me exactly what I have done wrong to deserve this ill treatment after all I tried to do to please you? Considering how much I love and care for you, I expect more of your attention. At least, you have the duty to grant me whatever I ask from you. I have a business appointment in Canada and I want to take you with me. Is that too much for me to ask from you?

ROSITA: *(goes to sit in another place.)* I am not leaving Nigeria for any reason. Period. I have some things to look after in my father's business just as you are looking after your father's.

AUGUSTINE: You probably forgot that you don't make certain decisions. Your father makes the decisions about both us. I've discussed the issue with him. He told me to take you with me.

ROSITA: *(laughs softly.)*You sound as if my father will tell you, not only me how to live our lives. *(She looks at him briefly.)* For one, I doubt if you believe that yourself. For two, I wonder what you take me for - a baby that needs people to decide for her... Come on, Augustine, give me a break. I'm getting sick of this.

AUGUSTINE: Going by the agreement between your family and mine, we are supposed to be doing things together by now.

ROSITA: We are not married. How would you expect me to do things together with you? Even if we are, marriage cannot be run with business. They are two different things. I keep telling you this but you are not listening.

AUGUSTINE: Let's talk about our marriage. We would have been married by now. You keep telling everyone that you are not ready.

ROSITA: Do me a favour, Augustine. Let's not bring up that issue.

AUGUSTINE: Are you still thinking we are not going to get married? *(There is silence.)* Now, listen, your parents and mine have agreed that we'll get married. Not only that, they have agreed that our businesses will be merged when we are married. Now you want to cancel that proposal?

ROSITA: We are not getting anywhere with this issue. So let's skip the issue of marriage for now, please.

AUGUSTINE: *(sighs.)* All right. Whatever your decision, I love you.

ROSITA: Thank you.

AUGUSTINE: I wonder when you're going to tell me you love me too.

ROSITA: I'll tell you if I sure I do. *(He stares at her for a moment before he leaves the room silently.)*

ACT ONE SCENE TWO

(There is a small party in Nelly's wide sitting room, celebrating the birthday with her. Martin sits and talks with Nelly. Rosita who is sitting far opposite them, watching the people around catches the sight of the two of them.)

NELLY: *(laughs.)* ...You don't have to tell Niyi about my age. He knows it. If he didn't know it before now, at least he knows that I'm celebrating my 23rd birthday today. So do yourself some good and stop gossiping around about my age.

MARTINS: *(looks round and sees Rosita looking them. He looks back at Nelly.)* Nelly, who's that beautiful lady looking at us over there. Don't look at her, please. She's in red long dress. She is sitting directly opposite us.

NELLY: *(steals a glance at Rosita.)* Oh, she's my big cousin. Her name is Rosita Daniel.

MARTINS: I like her looks. You don't mind if you introduce me to her, do you?

NELLY: Come off it, Martins. She is already engaged to a man.

MARTINS: People use to say ladies are caps. They stay on the head of men that fit them perfectly.

NELLY: What makes you think you fit her more than the guy she is engaged to?

MARTINS: Come on, sugar girl. You can never tell what I can offer her.

NELLY: *(bursts out laughing.)* You're a poor civil servant. I don't need to remind you of that, do I? You have nothing to offer her. You are no match for her at all because she is really a wealthy lady. It takes a wealthy man to love her. Boy, she's going to find you so distasteful because your monthly salary is not even enough to entertain her visitors in week.

MARTINS: *(frowns at her as she laughs at him.)* Now, now, Nelly, don't make me feel like a very wretched guy or ... Like... Em... a disgrace to you. Money is not what makes love, you know. It's the heart.

NELLY: *(laughs the more.)* How come you suddenly turn into a preacher that talks about what makes love? What do you know about love? Man! You've always said that poor guys are not reckoned with in the society.

MARTINS: Let's forget what I once said about being poor. So please introduce me to her. Baby, I'm desperate.

NELLY: *(giggles.)* All right, lover boy. *(She looks at Rosita who is now looking somewhere else. She gets her attention by waving at her. She beckons on her to come to sit with her. Rosita stands up and goes to join her, sitting beside her. She greets Martins with a smile and nod.)* Rosita, meet Martins, Niyi's best friend. I told you about Niyi, didn't I?

ROSITA: Oh, yeah. Niyi is your boyfriend in US. *(She smiles.)* I had the impression that he's … *(gestures at Martins.)* Niyi.

MARTINS: Oh no, I'm not her boyfriend. She finds me unsuitable because I'm a poor Civil Servant.*(Rosita chuckles.)* Niyi only told me to take care of her before leaving for United States so that guys out there do not mess around her. That's why I'm playing the role of a protective boyfriend.

ROSITA: *(smiles at him.)* I see. Anyway, how are you doing? *(She offers her hand in handshakes.)*

MARTINS: *(shakes hands with her.)* I am doing fine. It's nice to meet you, Rosita.

NELLY: *(stands up and straightens her skirts.)* You guys can keep each other's company while I attend to the guests. *(She leaves to join others.)*

ACT ONE SCENE THREE

(Still at the scene of the party within the premises. Martins walks with Rosita who is laughing whole heartedly. There is music playing at a distance in the house where the party is held.)

ROSITA: Martins, you're impossible! *(She laughs loudly.)*

MARTINS: I told the guys, "You really want to squeeze life out of me?

You took my money, you took my bicycle, you took my... my senses and you expect me to give you a good dance." You should have seen these guys. They really mean business. My sense was returned when I was beaten stupid. Before I knew it, I was already dancing like - you know how it feels to be dancing in such condition. *(Rosita continues to laugh*.) One of them played an imaginary guitar, another played a saxophone, another one beat a drum with his chest and the leader of the group sang one of Fella's songs about zombie. He said, "tell am to go straight, joro jara joro…" Before I knew it was a set up by someone I had offended in the class, I've given them all the various kinds of funny dance I knew including that of Zombie!

ROSITA: *(laughs and begins to cease.)*You had a bad influence when you were in school, right?

MARTINS: That's true. I could easily be influenced by the people I like. You see, the problem is I used to like the wrong people.

ROSITA: I hope you have changed now?

MARTINS: You know, I'm no longer a kid. I now influence other people positively. *(There was silence as they walk round slowly round the premises. He looks at her.)* Rosita, you know you are such a beautiful lady.

ROSITA: *(looks at him briefly.)* Thank you.

MARTINS: Are you offended by the remark?

ROSITA: Hmm, not really. Such expressions sometimes convey some impressions.

MARTINS: Impressions like what?

ROSITA: Never mind.

MARTINS: *(silently.)* Rosita, I'm not as an unmannerly as you are probably thinking.

ROSITA: Oh no, I don't have that impression at all, honestly.

MARTINS: It seems to me you're trying to draw a boundary. That really makes me feel uncomfortable with you. You are such a pleasant lady and I want to be free with you. Don't you want me to be free with you?

ROSITA: *(holds his hand silently.)* I'm very sorry if it seems to you as if I'm drawing a boundary. *(They stop walking.)* Perhaps I should erase that impression by saying that you're a very pleasant person to make friends with. You possess some virtues which I quite appreciate.

MARTINS: Come on, say that again. I really love be flattered, especially by someone like you. It makes me feel good. Come on, go ahead and flatter me the more.

ROSITA: *(laughs again.)* I'm not trying to flatter you. I'm only expressing my candid opinion about you.

MARTINS: Then it makes a whole lot of senses if we become close friends, isn't it?

ROSITA: Yes. But we are friends - just friends, Martins.

ACT ONE SCENE FOUR

ROSITA: *(Rosita is in her well furnished office, writing. The telephone intercom on the table rings. She picks it up)* Yes... Mr what? .... Oh, Martins, tell him to come in. *(Then she drops the telephone. A moment later, the door opens and Martins, dressed in a well tailored suit enters.)* Hay, Martins, how are you?

MARTINS: I'm fine, thanks.

ROSITA: *(waves to a seat. Martins sits down comfortably in front of her, crossing his legs. They look and smile at each other.)* You promised to give me a call last week but you fail to fulfil your promise.

MARTINS: And why didn't you call to find out why?

ROSITA: I was so busy that it never crossed my mind.

MARTINS: That's a proof that you think less of me each time we away from each other.

ROSITA: That's not true. Even if it is, you really can't blame me. I've got so much work here that I can hardly think of anything else. Where were you? I suppose you were not in town, am I right?

MARTINS: I was in Abuja through out the week. I arrived yesterday evening. The Director General informed me of an urgent meeting with the minister the day the plane was scheduled take off to the place. So I have to go with him without informing anyone.

ROSITA: This civil service work is not for those who love pleasure.

MARTINS: It's not the same with other sections. I guess it is the nature of my office.

ROSITA: I see.

MARTINS: I really missed your laugher.

ROSITA: *(smiles.)* I missed your company too. You know, I feel like listening to your anecdotes once in a while. What can we offer you? Coffee?

MARTINS: I need food because I'm starving.

ROSITA: I can't offer that to you in the office. You know that.

MARTINS: Then let's go and get it somewhere else.

ROSITA: I really can't go anywhere right now. I'm very busy. I can tell someone to take you to the restaurant where you can be treated with a great delicacy.

MARTINS: I'm not here to be treated with delicacy by someone else but you. If you are not taking me there yourself, I'm going home to sleep for one week.

ROSITA: *(laughs.)* Oh, no, Martins, not today, please. I'm so busy and the work is so urgent. *(He spreads her hand over the files and documents on the table.)* If I don't work on these, the company may lose a fortune. So please, be considerate.

MARTINS: Does any has anything to do with the Federal Government?

ROSITA: No. Why do you ask?

MARTINS: I thought your company is among those bidding for supply of some hardware at the Ministry of Agriculture.

ROSITA: I see. They all relate to the export of our products to the neighbouring countries like Ghana, Benin Republic. We've been looking for the opportunities for a long time.

MARTINS: All right, I'll let you off the hook for now but I'll like to see you at Nelly's house on Saturday in the evening if you don't mind.

ROSITA: *(looks at her organizer on the table.)* Let me see where I'm supposed to be around then... Oh, Martins, I'll be having a meeting with someone in Victoria Island.

MARTINS: The meeting would have ended before evening.

ROSITA: I have no idea how long it will last.

MARTINS: I'm not going to accept that, Rosita. I want to see you on Saturday. It's really important that we see.

ROSITA: *(looks at him for a while. He stares back at her.)* You're one hell of a domineering person, aren't you?

MARTINS: You can say that again. *(He smiles. She smiles with him. After a while, he stands up to go.)* I'll be there by six p.m. By then you would have completed every assignment for that day.

ROSITA: All right. I'll see you then.

MARTINS: Cheers. *(He leaves the office, smiling at her.)*

ACT ONE SCENE FIVE

(Martins is pacing up and down in Nelly's sitting room with Rosita sitting on the couch, looking at him as he walks around.)

MARTINS: What I'm about to say is something you probably guessed. Actually, I'm not a smooth operator but I do have feelings like every other normal person…

ROSITA: Now, Martins…

MARTINS: I'll do the talking if you don't mind. *(He walks closer to look at her in the face.)* You are a very beautiful lady and very rich - those are enough to drive any man crazy but I'm not crazy about that. You may choose to withdraw your friendship with me after telling you the way I feel about you. I simply don't care…. *(Rosita frowns at him.)* You really think you can frighten me with that expression on your face? No way, baby. No way. I'll still express myself anyway even if you punch me in the face. As you can see, I'm helplessly in love with you. *(Rosita looks irritated.)* Since the day I meet you, I kept falling in love with you every time we see. You see, true love cannot be threatened or intimidated by anything, not even by the dangerous way you are staring at me now. I was afraid you will turn me down but I'm not afraid to take the chance to tell you that I really love you. Rosita, I love you. You've stolen my heart the very day I saw you. If you don't want me to lose my sleep over that, please, I beg of you, just say you love me even if I'm too poor for you to marry. *(Rosita unexpectedly bursts into prolonged laughter)*

ROSITA: I knew you can never be serious. You have never been serious even once. Martins, the joker, Martins, the orator. You should have been an actor, you know. *(Martins looks at her for a long time. Then he grips her and attempts to kiss her. She pulls away and goes to sit in another place)* Are you out of your mind?

MARTINS: You said I'm not serious. I want to convince you that I am.

ROSITA: We had a deal, don't we? We are just friends. Let's leave it at that level.

MARTINS: No! I decide what I from you. You are not to tell me what you want from me.

ROSITA: *(looks serious.)* So this is what you had in mind all along.

MARTINS: Yes!

ROSITA: Do you know what I think?

MARTINS: Yeah?

ROSITA: I think you are out of your mind.

MARTINS: You really think I'm out of my mind? *(He looks frustrated.)* You think I'm out of my mind because I love you. What a mess.

ROSITA: Martins, this is going too far. We agreed to be just friends when we started this, didn't we?

MARTINS: *(let out a deep breath.)* You have to forget about that. I never meant this to be mere friendship. Nelly knows this.

ROSITA: *(frowns at him.)* And she encouraged you?

MARTINS: Please, let's not bring her into this, in case things get pretty messy. I'm acting alone here, okay?

ROSITA: Martins, the truth is: it's not possible for us to be in love.

MARTINS: That's interesting. That's the first time I'm going to hear that it's not possible for two people to be in love.

ROSITA: Can't you understand? We are two different people meant for different people.

MARTINS: I still don't understand the point.

ROSITA: The point is I belong to another man and you belong to another lady. We don't belong to each other. That is the point.

MARTINS: What makes people belong to each other? Money? *(There is silence. He smiles ruefully.)* I see the point now.

ROSITA: What you see is not the point. The point is you cannot claim you don't have a lover, can you?

MARTINS: I have a lover but she knows I cannot marry her.

ROSITA: You can't marry the lady you call your lover. Why are you befriending her in the first place? Are you a playboy or something?

MARTINS: I'm not. I'm just looking for the right person to love. If I love a lady, I'll marry her because love is the only foundation every good home can be built. I want to have a good home.

ROSITA: You cannot have me, Martins, because I'm not yours.

MARTINS: Why not? You don't love me. *(There is silence.)* That's the most hurtful thing in my life. I never imagine I'll fall in love with a lady who never cares a bit about me. *(He moves closer to hers.)* Rosita, you're a murderer! You deliberately gave me the impression that you loved me so that I can fall in love with you. Now that you have my heart in your hand, you decide to break it. I wish I know what you hope to achieve in doing this to me. Well, You can kill me emotionally because you've got me where you want me. Kill my emotion, brutalize my feelings for you, destroy my joy - do whatever you like if it makes you happy. You want to see me cry? I'll disappoint you because I'm not going to cry, at least, not when you are there to laugh at me. Mind you... *(He points at her.)* I won't forgive you for this and I don't ever want to set my eyes on you again - ever! *(He backs away slowly, looking at her grieved expressions.)*

ROSITA: *(looks away from him for a moment. She looks at him quietly.)* You get it all wrong, Martins. I … *(Martins waves indifferently, indicating that he does not want to hear her explanations. He walks out of the room, slamming the door behind him. Rosita sits still, looking at the door. After a moment, tears begin to drop from her eyes. Then Nelly enters the room from the back.)*

NELLY: *(looks at Rosita as she stares at the door. She walks closer to her, sits beside her and taps her gently. Rosita does not move until she pulls her to her directions.)* Rosita, what's the matter? Come on, talk to me, big cousin.

ROSITA: I think I … hurt Martins and he hurts me. *(She dries her tears.)*

NELLY: Tell me what happened.

ROSITA: He was…em… trying to explain how much he loves me. He… em told I'm a murderer. He said he gave me his heart and I broke it. He thought I made him fall in love with him so that I can destroy his joy. *(She shakes her head, looking guilty.)* I've never seen him looking so hurt and frustrated. I wish I can put back his smiles… I feel so sorry for him.

NELLY: *(holds her hand gently.)* Oh, dear Rosita, you are not feeling sorry for him.

ROSITA: *(looks more grieved.)* I really feel sorry for him. What could have made me cry if I don't? I mean - you should have seen his face. For a moment, I thought he was going to cry. I… really can't help blaming myself for making our friendship go this far.

NELLY: You couldn't help it. You told me that yourself, remember?

ROSITA: I should have told him about Augustine. Perhaps that would have put a check on our relationship.

NELLY: And you think that would have stopped both of you from getting this far?

ROSITA: I'm not sure I understand your thoughts, Nelly.

NELLY: I don't expect you to understand my thoughts because you don't seem to understand your own feelings. If you can answer this question sincerely I mean sincerely, you will not only understand my thoughts but also your own feelings. The question is: how do you feel so sorry to the extent of crying for a man you don't really love. Augustine went through much more psychological pain in your relationship with him than Martins yet you never feel sorry for him. Rosita, the truth is: you are in love with Martins. You don't feel so sorry for someone you don't love.

ROSITA: *(sighs)* Actually, I'm afraid to admit that. I feel it but I thought the feelings will go the way it came. Even Martins knows I love him but he thought I just gave him that impression so that I can break his heart. Even then, you know there is nothing we can do about it.

37

I'm engaged to Augustine. Only God can stop our marriage. If God does not intervene in the marriage plan, I'm already his wife. I shouldn't be telling you this because you know exactly what is going on. I must also confess to you that I was surprised you encouraged Martins to go this far with me, knowing fully well what it takes to be so involved with me.

NELLY: I didn't really encourage him. He only asked me to introduce him to you on my birthday which I did. Even then, you know that once the rope of love is tied by whatever, nobody, as a matter of fact, can untie it.

ROSITA: *(smiles.)* Hay, that makes sense. Where do you learn it from?

NELLY: I have no idea where it came from but I'm glad it put smiles on your face.

ROSITA: What do you suggest I do now? I don't think I'll have some peace until I do something about Martins' feelings for me. You know my parents and Augustine's proposed that we get married for mutual and business interests.

NELLY: You must not think of the interest of your business or other things when picking someone you are going to spend the rest of your life with. You have to think of love and trust which are the bedrock of every good family set up. If you build your family set up on business interest, it will collapse like a house of cards. But if you build it on true love, there will be peace, harmony and joy. These are what you need for goodness sake.

ROSITA: You are right but would my parents see things that way? More so that Augustine had blindfolded everyone with everything he used to do for my family. Through him, we've won several contracts with both State and federal governments.

NELLY: What you need to ask yourself is: do you love Augustine? Other things are secondary and sentimental issues.

ROSITA: You know I don't love Augustine even though I tried to. The more I tried to love him, the more I see so many things I don't like about him.

NELLY: How about your feelings for Martins?

ROSITA: He's a pleasant and jovial guy who seems to know how to make me very happy. No doubt, I can spend the rest of my life with him.

NELLY: Then you don't need anyone to tell you who to pitch your tent with.

ROSITA: What about the problem with my parents? Besides,

Augustine may stop at nothing but to deal with anyone that tries to get involved with me.

NELLY: I can see your point but I don't exactly see it as a problem. Just tell Martins the problem and see if there is something he can do about it. That is the best thing you can do for now.

ACT TWO SCENE ONE

(Chief Daniel is sitting opposite Augustine in Chief Daniel's house.)

AUGUSTINE: Really, sir, she had not been paying much attention to me. I remember the time you advised me to ask her if she would like to travel with me to Canada and how she refused my request.

CHIEF DANIEL: *(smiles.)* She's probably afraid she'll swallow a baby if she stayed with you for two weeks.

AUGUSTINE: She is not the type of lady that any man can mess around with. I mean - she'll not even sit on the same chair with me, let alone to touch or sleep in the same room with me. So I don't think that's her reason. I'm afraid there is something else.

CHIEF DANIEL: And what do you suspect is happening?

AUGUSTINE: I have a good reason to believe she is going contrary to what we proposed.

CHIEF DANIEL: What gives you that idea?

AUGUSTINE: *(shrugs.)* Considering the delay she had caused in the marriage so far and her attitude towards me, I'm forced to suspect that she is involved with someone else.

CHIEF DANIEL: You are wrong, you know.

AUGUSTINE: I stand to be corrected, sir. She may not give you that impression but …

CHIEF DANIEL: *(goes to pat him on the shoulder.)* She is a career girl who loves to do things in her own way but I can assure you that you are going to get married to each sooner than you think.

AUGUSTINE: *(looks hopeful.)* I look forward to that time, sir.

CHIEF DANIEL: I'll work towards that.

ACT TWO SCENE TWO

(Martins stands by the window in his office, looking absentmindedly. After a moment, his secretary enters the office with some documents. Martins does not move from his position. The secretary clears her throat. Martins remains where he is.)

SECRETARY: The DG sent these to us, sir. *(There is silence.)* He wants you to make some recommendations on each …

MARTINS: *(interrupts her.)* Leave them on the table.

SECRETARY: Okay, sir. *(She places them on the table and begins to move towards the door. She stops by the door and looks at him. He remains where he is.)* Is anything wrong, sir?

MARTINS: There is nothing. I'm just not in the mood to do or say anything.

SECRETARY: I've never seen you like this. Is there anything I can do?

MARTINS: Just leave me alone, please.

SECRETARY: I'm sorry to border you, sir. *(She starts moving again)*

MARTINS: Miss Farrot. *(She stops to look at him. He turns to look at her.)* I don't mean to shun you. I'm just tensed up. I'll get over it.

SECRETARY: I'm sure you will.

MARTINS: *(smiles at her.)* Thanks. You are always caring.

SECRETARY: *(returns the smiles.)* Thanks for the complements. *(As she goes out, Martins goes to sit behind his table to look at the documents. He studies the documents for sometime before his mobile phone begins to ring. He looks at it before he receives the call.)*

MARTINS: Hello, Nelly… Niyi called you? When...? I see… I may not be able to come down there to get it …Why don't you send the message to me if they are so important and urgent…? All right, I'll drive down there when I'm coming from the office. I hope you will be around then… All right, I'll see you then. *(He drops the phone on the table and continues to study the documents.)*

ACT TWO SCENE THREE A

(Rosita is with Nelly, sitting beside each other as they talk)

NELLY: You can easily tell if a guy is nice in the way he opens up to you although some may deliberately irritate you to test your temperament. I remember the time I met Niyi. We were having a seminar inside one of the lecture halls at University of Lagos while studying for the Master's Degree. *(She looks as if she is trying to recollect the topic.)* The topic was Conflict Resolution. I will never forget it. He was in the Physics Department, also running the Master's Programme. He came to sit beside me. I think he did that on purpose because he was sitting somewhere else before he changed his position to my side. I didn't need to be told that he has something in his mind but I wondered how he would succeed getting my attention because for one, I don't appreciate lousy or impatient guys. He has similar ways of making jokes like Martins. When one of the speakers introduced the topic of the paper he was to deliver: International Peace Settlement, he muttered, 'I wonder how that would be possible with so much greed around the world.' I almost chuckled but I just thought he must be a lousy guy. When the lecture ended, he asked if he could help me carry the only two

41

books I was holding, I told him not to border. You know what he said? *(Rosita smiles, shaking her head.)* He said, 'you see why I said peace settlement would not be possible in this world. I am just trying to put one of the things we learned into practice and you made it fail. Why wouldn't it fail, when we are always suspicious of one another?' I just laughed. From there, you know, we became familiar until he proposed to marry me. That was long before he travelled out of Nigeria.

ROSITA: How did you come across Martins?

NELLY: Niyi introduced him to me few days after we met. They were always together even though Martins was doing his Master's Degree at Lagos State University. You should have seen the two of them together. They were always joking about everything. They never seem serious at all… *(The door bell rings.)* I think he is the one. *(She goes to open the door. Martins waits by the door. She smiles at him.)* Hello, Martins.

MARTINS: *(smiles.)* Hi. I'm afraid I don't have much time.

NELLY: *(waves him inside, smiling.)* You will have to spare some minutes. Please, come in. *(Martins walks slowly inside the sitting room as Nelly closes the door.)* You can have your seat. *(Martins stops short when he sees Rosita. He turns to look at Nelly briefly before he goes to sit opposite Rosita silently.)* What can I offer you?

MARTINS: Nothing. Just get me the parcel from Niyi and I'm out of here.

NELLY: *(looks at Rosita who is looking at him. Then she looks at Martins who is looking at the window.)* Is anything the matter between the two of you? You behave as if you are total strangers. Even if you are strangers, courtesy demands that you at least greet each other. *(She looks at Rosita.)* What is the matter, Rosita?

ROSITA: I think you should ask him. If he doesn't feel like talking to me, why should I talk to him first?

NELLY: *(looks at Martins.)* Martins, what is the matter? Are you having anything against my cousin?

MARTINS: You ladies must have considered me a fool. You expect me to believe she didn't tell you what happened?

NELLY: You tell me what happened.

MARTINS: I have not come for that here. I believe you have a message for me. Give it to me and let me get out of this place.

NELLY: Martins, if you are fighting my cousin, you are fighting me. You are not going anywhere until you have iron out your differences.

I'm going to prepare some food now while you settle your quarrel.

MARTINS: *(stands)* Wait a minute, Nelly. I told you I don't have much time.

NELLY: Well, you can find another time to come and get it.

MARTINS: You're holding me to a ransom, right?

NELLY: Whatever.

ROSITA: Martins, sit down and let's talk. You may not have any reason to blame me after all. *(Martins looks at her for a moment.)* Sit down, please. *(Martins sits down slowly.)*

NELLY: What would you like me to make for you?

MARTINS: I had a heavy lunch in the office.

NELLY: Then I can make you light meal - your favourite?

MARTINS: All right if it makes you happy. *(Nelly smiles at both of them as she goes to the kitchen. There is a brief silence.)*

ROSITA: Why did you consider me a murderer, Martins?

MARTINS: I am sorry for that. But you have to understand one thing. For the first time in my entire life, I'm defeated b my feelings for a lady. I never thought this is the way love exists. I kept fighting it everywhere at home, in the office everywhere. What really hurts is the feeling that you don't care about the way I feel.

ROSITA: I never tell you I don't care, did I?

MARTINS: *(goes to sit down beside her.)* Perhaps there is something I should know about your feelings which I don't know.

ROSITA: The problem with you is that you jump into conclusions. If you think I don't care for you or your feelings, you are wrong. It may interest you if I confess that Nelly arranged this meeting. You don't have any message from Niyi as she claimed. She felt that is the only way I can get the chance to explain some things to you. When I finish telling you, you'll have the ball in your court. You can play it as you like. First, you must understand that I was all along trying to protect you by trying as much as I can to prevent our friendship from growing into the kind of relationship you want it to be. I couldn't prevent it for obvious reason.

MARTINS: What's the obvious reason if I may ask?

ROSITA: Let me explain what is happening first. *(She looks thoughtful as scene changes with the big close up of her face)*

ACT TWO SCENE FOUR
(Flashback)

(Chief Daniel, Dr Cole, Augustine and Mrs Daniel are in Daniel's' sitting room as they discuss.)

43

DR COLE: My son, Augustine had always admired Rosita since they met at the cocktail party during your company's anniversary two years ago. I'm sure you remember what happened that day.

CHIEF DANIEL: Oh yes, I can't forget that day. *(He smiles.)* I cannot readily forget the trick you and your son played on my daughter that day. You requested him to dance with her and created the impression that they were in love.

DR COLE: *(laughs.)* Actually, it wasn't my idea. It was Augustine's.

MRS DANIEL: It worked anyway. Ever since then, it was as if both of them are brother and sister.

DR COLE: Yes, but Augustine wants to extend the relationship beyond that.

CHIEF DANIEL: I wish I understand what you mean by that.

DR COLE: Oh, there is... *(He looks at Augustine.)* I think you're in the better position to say your mind.

AUGUSTINE: Actually, Chief, I love Rosita very much. I have no doubt she likes me though she never expressed this in anyway. I feel... em... she will...em... make a good wife. I, therefore, want to propose that you give her to my in marriage. I promise to take very good care of her.

DR COLE: Besides that, the companies of both families can have good relationship if they get married.

CHIEF DANIEL: *(looks thoughtful.)* That sounds like a good idea, especially if we consider the fact that Rosita who, as you know, is our only daughter, needs a loving man as husband. But you know, as the saying goes, you cannot shave a man's head without his consent. You go ahead and make the proposal known to her. We can try to influence her decision through our counsel. That's the best we can do.

DR COLE: We'll really appreciate that

MRS DANIEL: You can give us time to talk to her first before you make the proposal to her. *(The flashback returns to scene eight.)*

ACT TWO SCENE THREE B

ROSITA: ... My parents discussed the issue together, laying more emphasis on what the family tends to gain than what I will gain in the marriage with Augustine. I wouldn't blame them because no one knew Augustine is egocentric until I discover this few months ago. In fact, that is what made me very reluctant to go into marriage with him. Up till now, my parents still believe he is a man of perfect virtue. He lavish presents on everyone and used his powerful connection to win us so many big contracts that helped my father's companies to flourish. At the beginning, I consented to be his girlfriend until I am sure of the kind of person he is. I discover so many things I don't like about him. When he continues to press me for marriage, I told him I'm not yet ready for that now. He went to my parents and persuaded them to talk me into getting married to him soonest. They told him to agree on the date of the marriage with me. He came to my house one day and… *(She looks thoughtful again as the scene changes into another flashback.)*

ACT TWO SCENE FIVE
(Flashback)

(Augustine is pacing round Rosita's sitting room while Rosita looks at him)

AUGUSTINE: …. Your parents and my parents have agreed that we can get married. They want us to pick a date.

ROSITA: *(looks puzzled.)* What are you talking about here, Augustine?

AUGUSTINE: I'm talking about marriage.

ROSITA: Whose marriage?

AUGUSTINE: The marriage between you and me.

ROSITA: Who is planning about marriage with you?

AUGUSTINE: And what does that mean?

ROSITA: You not in the position to ask me that question. In fact, you own me an explanation why you are doing this. Why are you so desperate? You've been going to my parents to talk about marriage without seeking for my consent first. Do you really believe you can succeed with that kind of plans?

AUGUSTINE: Rosita, this is the desire of your family and mine. I am not desperate. Even if I am, call it love.

ROSITA: *(snorts.)* This is not love. This is something else. And this is not the desire of anyone but yours. You're trying to make it theirs.

AUGUSTINE: *(sighs.)* All right, it is my desire because I love you very much. I know you do love me too. So why can't we…

ROSITA: What makes you think I love you and what makes you think you are in love with me and not infatuated.

AUGUSTINE: I love you, Rosita. You need to encourage me by saying you love me too.

ROSITA: I'm not sure I do and I don't want to rush into marriage with you since I'm not yet sure of whom you are or what you really want from me?

AUGUSTINE: *(goes on his kneels.)* All I want from you is your love. If there is anything that make me so desperate have you, it is the love I have for you. Look... if you don't love and marry me, I'm a dead man.

ROSITA: I'm not sure this is what they call love. So give me time to think about, would you?

ACT TWO SCENE THREE C

ROSITA: ... Even at that point, I just wanted him to leave me alone. I don't really plan to think about anything because, he's too desperate for my liking. Such a man can be clouded with insane jealousy if he sees his woman with male friends.

After waiting a long time for my response, he went to my parents to tell them I was breaking his heart. He was able to arouse sympathy for himself. My mother sent for me and had an argument with me which invariably indicates that my parents would never be on my side if I decide not to get married to Augustine…

ACT TWO SCENE SIX
(Flashback)

(Mrs Daniel stands in front of Rosita who sits in Chief Daniel's sitting room.)

MRS DANIEL: Come on, young lady, teach me what I don't know about love. You don't even have another man in your life, let alone loving him. Even if you have a man you think you love, there is no way he can be as virtuous as Augustine. Love has eyes to see what is good in a man. If what you think is love does not have eyes, you let it your own eyes and see that the best man for you is Augustine.

ROSITA: Can I ask you one question, mum?

MRS DANIEL: Go ahead.

ROSITA: Did you marry my father for what he is or for what he has?

MRS DANIEL: What sort of question is that? You really think I can be enticed by material possession?

ROSITA: That does not answer my question.

MRS DANIEL: I married your father because he is a nice person and I knew he would take care of me.

ROSITA: You mean you didn't marry him because you love him.

MRS DANIEL: Love came later, Rosita. It came after we got married. It will come in your own case too if you give it a chance by getting married.

ROSITA: Love might have come later in your case probably because you and my father understand each other. It may not come in my case. I am not prepared to take the risk of getting married to the man I don't love.

MRS DANIEL: Don't throw away your gold in the mud. You may not find it again. Any lady would do anything to get married to Augustine.

ROSITA: I'm not any lady, Mum. I'm not looking for what any lady would look for in a man. I need a man that will make me happy - a man that I love and who loves me, not a man that is desperate to get what he wants by any means.

MRS DANIEL: That's not fair, Rosita! You can't say a thing like that against someone who has done so much for the family

ROSITA: *(stands up suddenly.)* That is the point! I'm bought and paid for by someone whose true colour is hidden from you.

MRS DANIEL: What exactly do you mean by that? You agreed to be his girlfriend in the first place, didn't you? Tell me if you didn't!

ROSITA: Augustine is not the nice guy we all think. He just wants me by all means and that's all…

ACT TWO SCENE THREE D

ROSITA: ... There is no way I can possibly convince anyone that all Augustine wants is me. If he is able to get me, my parents would see his true colour. I waited to get them a proof of what I mean until…hmmm… I'm not sure if I should tell you this…

MARTINS: Why not? I need to hear everything.

ROSITA: *(There is silence.)* Augustine can be very brutal if he suspects that I'm involved with anyone. He sent some guys to beat up one of my mates in secondary school just because he discovered that the guy was interested in me. That was the proof I needed to give to my parents but no one believe he was such a person. So I challenged him myself when he came to me as usual…

ACT TWO SCENE SEVEN
(Flashback)

(Flashback. Rosita and Augustine stand in front of each other exchanging words.)

ROSITA: You should be ashamed of yourself for beating up a man like that because of a woman.

AUGUSTINE: Who did I beat?

ROSITA: Sometimes I wonder if you truly believe I have no sense at

47

all. You want to deny you have nothing to do with one of my class mates that was beaten mercilessly.

AUGUSTINE: I don't have the slightest idea of what you are talking about.

ROSITA: The description of the men that beat up the guy fit the men I've seen with you. So give me another story.

AUGUSTINE: Believe me; I don't have anything to do with it. Come to think of it, are you going out with a man?

ACT TWO SCENE THREE E

ROSITA: *...* If I tell him I'm going out with a man, he may become brutal enough to deal with anyone he suspects as my date. So I have to give him the impression that I'll still marry him even though I knew I will never marry him even if he's the only man remaining in the world. If I have not done that, you would have probably been in danger. *(There is silence as she looks thoughtful.)* Ever since I discovered the kind of person he is, he's been building himself the reputation of a very nice guy. He gives my parents and me expensive presents some of which I have to reject. Each time I reject his present, he would go to my parents to tell them I'm breaking his heart by rejecting the presents. *(There is another silence as she looks at Martins who looks thoughtful.)* All the while you think I don't care about you, I was in fact trying to protect you. *(She touches his forehead silently and draws a imaginary line with her finger.)* Martins, the day I met you and discovered the qualities in you, I became a very fearful person because I knew this type of thing would happen. I tried, God knows I tried to discourage you but like Nelly told me, once the rope of love is tied by whatever, it cannot be untied. *(In a whisper)* I tried to block you out of my life but I couldn't. I'm always thinking of you because…

MARTINS: *(In the same whisper.)* Because of what?

ROSITA: *(smiles.)* You already know.

MARTINS: Pleas, spell it out all the same.

ROSITA: I love you, Martins. There is no use hiding it from you again. *(She stands up.)* I must warn you that our feelings for each other can land us into big trouble.

MARTINS: I'm ready to pay the price and get you out of it - just for myself.

ROSITA: The ransom for my love for you is high, Martins.

MARTINS: *(stands up to face her, holding her both hands.)* I'll pay it, not matter how high.

ROSITA: *(looks at his face with smiles and she whispers.)* I suppose you want to kiss me.

MARTINS: *(In whispers.)* Yes. Can I? *(She nods. As he moves his mouth to hers, the door to the kitchen opens and Nelly comes out. They stop to look at her.)*

NELLY: *(puts some plates on the table without looking at them.)* Believe me, I don't see what is going on here. So go ahead and do whatever you want to do. *(Martins and Rosita laugh.)*

MARTINS: Naughty girl!

ACT THREE SCENE ONE

(Rosita parks her car in front of Martins' house and goes to press the door bell. While waiting for the door to open, another car is parked some meters away from Rosita's car. Augustine and Dele stay in the car, looking at Rosita. A moment later, Martins opens the door, smiles at Rosita who offers her cheek to him. He kisses her cheek and leads her inside the house. Augustine looks angry.)

AUGUSTINE: *(glances at Dele.)* What's she doing here?

DELE: How the hell am I supposed to know? I only observe she comes here each time she is coming from the office. The first day I saw her car, I thought she probably came to visit a friend or something but when I saw her about four or five times, I began to feel something is going on there. *(There is silence.)*

AUGUSTINE: *(looks at Martins' house for a long time.)* What do you think is going on inside that house?

DELE: You don't need anyone to tell you, do you? *(There is silence.)* Really, Austin, I don't go around, poking my nose into another man's business but I consider you a good business partner and I can't possibly see what your fiancée is involved in without telling you.

AUGUSTINE: Tell me exactly what you think is happening, Dele.

DELE: Like I said, you don't need anyone to tell you what is happening inside. You just saw them kissing, didn't you?.

AUGUSTINE: The kissing on the cheek may not mean that much.

DELE: My friend, let's face the truth. There is something between the two of them.

AUGUSTINE: *(clutches his fix and mutters.)* I'll crush the guy without efforts. *(He shoots a glance at Dele.)* Who is guy anyway?

DELE: As I gathered, he's one of the top guys in the Ministry of Works and Housing - the deputy director.

AUGUSTINE: I see… He feels he can mess around with my fiancée because he's a top guy in the civil service. *(There is another silence. Then he opens the car door.)* I'm going to deal with him.

DELE: Man, are you nuts? If you do a thing like that, you will be in trouble.

AUGUSTINE: Me? In trouble?

DELE: You don't know what I mean. Your family and fiancée's will never take side with you if you strike him now.

AUGUSTINE: *(sits back into the car.)* This is deep shit, man! Surely,

50

that guy must not go away with that. He couldn't be sleeping with her ...Oh, shit! This same girl that goes about with another man will not even allow me to even touch her. This is real shit, man!

DELE: You have to calm down otherwise you'll find yourself in a mess. The whole world would see you as hooligan that beats up a man because of a woman.

AUGUSTINE: I don't care!

DELE: You better care because that can make you lose the girl completely.

AUGUSTINE: *(looks thoughtful.)* I should have known this all along. She was not thinking of getting married to me. She wanted to get married to that guy.

DELE: Feeling so jealous does not get us anywhere, man. Even if you want to teach the guy any sense, it would be foolish to do it by yourself. You have to send some guys that are not known to Rosita.

AUGUSTINE: Well, you can lead the men to the house, beat him out of shape and warn to stay clear off my fiancée.

DELE: What makes you think they will not trace the incident to you?

AUGUSTINE: I don't give a damn. So long the guy is beaten out of his wit.

DELE: Well, if you insist, the best we can do is to warn him after doing what you want and give him the impression that Rosita has many boyfriends. At least, it's better than going down there to beat the guy up yourself.

AUGUSTINE: All right, you'll handle him for me. *(A moment later, they drive away.)*

ACT THREE SCENE TWO

(Augustine waits in the car, a little far away from Rosita's house, watching the house. After sometime, Rosita drives into the premises. The security guard opens the gate after peeping to see who is coming in. Augustine continues to watch her as she waves at the guard. After sometime, Augustine drives into the premises. He horns and waits for the guard to reopen the gate. He again opens the gate after seeing him. Augustine greets him briefly.)

AUGUSTINE: How are you, Jude?

JUDE: I'm fine, sir. Thank you. *(Augustine drives inside and parks behind Rosita's car which is in front of the entrance. He gets out of the car and goes to press the door bell. The house maid comes to open the door.)*

HOUSE MAID: Welcome, sir.

AUGUSTINE: Thank you. *(He goes pass her into the sitting room and climbs the staircase and goes straight to Rosita's bed room while the house maid looks puzzled. He opens her bedroom without warning. Rosita sits on the bed, removing her shoes. She looks startled to see him.)* Hello, Rosita.

ROSITA: *(stands up slowly.)* Hello... W-what are you doing here?

AUGUSTINE: *(locks the door behind him.)* I've come to see you.

ROSITA: Why must you come to see me in my bedroom and why are you locking the door?

AUGUSTINE: I've come to have some fun with you, baby.

ROSITA: You know better than to play foul game with me, don't you?

AUGUSTINE: *(moves towards her slowly as she draws backward until she stops by the bed.)* We are due to marry, aren't we? So let's have it - now.

ROSITA: Have what?

AUGUSTINE: Let's have some fun or whatever you call it.

ROSITA: I'm not a cheap whore.

AUGUSTINE: Did I say you are? Come on, baby, give it to me.

ROSITA: Augustine, back off! You are out of your mind. *(He gives her a hard slap. She screams with pains. He pushes her on the bed and begins to remove his shirt.)*

AUGUSTINE: I'm going to have some fun with you right now.

ROSITA: *(jumps out of the bed.)* If you dare touch me, I swear I'll bite you and... I'll scream and I'll tell the whole world you try to rape me and... that will be the end of whatever is between us.

AUGUSTINE: *(calms down almost immediately.)* I'm sorry.

ROSITA: You better be. *(She points at the door.)* Open that damn door and get out of my room!

AUGUSTINE: *(goes to open the door.)* Well...em ... I guess I have to go and wait for you in the sitting room. *(He goes out. Rosita gives a sigh of relief.)*

ACT THREE SCENE THREE

(Martins is in his sitting room, reading when the door bell rings.)

MARTINS: The door is opened. *(Dele opens the door and enters the sitting room with two violent looking men. All the men wear sunglasses. Martins looks at them for a moment as they look at him.)* Can I help you, guys?

DELE: *(moves closer to him.)* You have offended someone and he has sent us to teach a lesson - just one good lesson you will live to remember for the rest of your miserable life.

MARTINS: Who sent you if I may ask?

DELE: We don't need to tell you that but he is one of the boyfriends of the ladies you are messing around with.

MARTINS: I may not be the guy you are looking for. You see, I don't mess around with ladies. *(He looks thoughtful for a moment.)* Wait a minute. You are sent here by Augustine, right?

DELE: *(There is silence.)* Wrong. See now, you don't even know that the lady you are messing around has many boyfriends. We are to teach all her boyfriends lessons. Are you ready for your lesson?

MARTINS: You listen to me. It's of no use if you guys bring violence into this matter. Do you think beating up men because of a lady who is loose is best way to handle this matter? If you hurt me now and because of that, I jilt her... *(He shrugs.)* That will not stop her from hooking up with other guys, going by what you said. For how long will you continue to do that? I think she is the problem here, not the guys. You can solve the problem through her, not through violence.

DELE: You are really a smart guy, aren't you? You sure know how to talk your way out of trouble but quite unfortunately, we have not come here to listen to nice speeches. *(He nods at the men who begin to beat Martins up. Martins tries to fight back but the men are too strong for him. So they beat him until he rolls on the floor with pains. After a while, the men leave. Martins craws slowly to the telephone. He manages to get his mobile phone to make a call.)*

MARTINS: Hello… Rosita… Please, come over to my house… Nothing very serious… Please, come as soon as you can. I just need you… Now…I'll be waiting… *(A moment later, he drops the phone and lies down on the floor.)*

ACT THREE SCENE FOUR

(Augustine sits in his house, drinking some wine, looking into some files on the table when Dele comes in.)

AUGUSTINE: *(looks up at him as he comes in.)* You are welcome. *(He gestures him to a seat.)* Do you mind some drinks? *(He goes to get a glass cup before he answers and pours out the drinks for him. Dele lets out a deep breath as he sits down.)* How does it go?

DELE: I just wondered if we have not made a mistake by doing what we did to the guy.

AUGUSTINE: Why do you say so?

DELE: The guy knows you. He asked us if you were the one that sent us.

AUGUSTINE: That's impossible! Rosita must have told him about me. How come?

DELE: How am I supposed to know? I told him you are not the one that sent us but one of Rosita's numerous boyfriends. Like I told you, I had hoped to create the impression that she has many boyfriends.

AUGUSTINE: What if he doesn't believe you?

DELE: *(shrugs.)* I'm afraid, that's your funeral. I told you initially that you don't have to teach the guy any lesson if you still want to have your woman back but you insisted.

AUGUSTINE: But you told me that was the best idea.

DELE: Now, don't push the blame to me. I said it was better than you going to beat the guy up yourself. I didn't encourage you to beat the guy. Besides, I didn't know that he knows you. If I had known, I would have completely discouraged it.

AUGUSTINE: Oh shit! What do we do now? If Rosita traces the beating to me, that's another big step forward in losing her to the guy completely. We've got to do something to ruin their relationship.

DELE: Assuming we have not touched the guy now, we could set up a lady to ruin their relationship.

AUGUSTINE: How?

DELE: We'll pay a lady to find a way to hook up with the guy and, you know, lure him to make love with her at the time Rosita would find them in the act.

AUGUSTINE: You should have thought of this in the first place.

DELE: I just thought of it while coming.

AUGUSTINE: What makes you think it will not work now?

DELE: The act can still be traced to you, especially if it happens shortly after the beatings.

AUGUSTINE: Let's give it a trial.

DELE: We'll have to wait for the heat of the beating to cool off before we implement the idea.

AUGUSTINE: *(drinks out of his glass)* All right, we'll do that.

DELE: *(looks thoughtful for a while.)* Augustine, please, let me ask you this question.

AUGUSTINE: Go ahead.

DELE: What is so special about this girl that is making you go this far? I mean a man of your calibre get any lady you want without stress. Something tells me there is more to what you're doing right now.

AUGUSTINE: *(signs.)* You're right, man. There is more to it. It's not about marriage with her per se. It's all about business though no one, not even my parents know this.

DELE: *(looks more thoughtful.)* I see...

AUGUSTINE: If only I can get her to marry me... *(He shrugs.)* We'll have our business interests merged. Of course, I'll seat over the companies as the chairman...

ACT THREE SCENE FIVE

(Martins sits on the floor in his sitting room, leaning his back against the couch, cleaning the blood on his arm and nose with a small handkerchief. After a moment, Rosita opens the door and comes in. She is looks frantic as she looks around the sitting room. She sees Martins on the floor and rushes to him.)

ROSITA: Martins! *(She quickly sits on the couch beside him.)* What happened? You need a doctor! *(She reaches out for her phone.)* I'll call the doctor now.

MARTINS: No, that won't be necessary. I can take care of myself or you take care of me.

ROSITA: Who did this to you?

MARTINS: Augustine. He has struck as you expected.

ROSITA: *(looks stunned.)* Oh my God...! *(Her surprised expression turns into thoughtful looks.)* No wonder...

MARTINS: No wonder what?

ROSITA: He tried to rape me. He has never make such attempt before now.

MARTINS: I see. The man who led other men said you have many boyfriends. I didn't believe him anyway. I guess it is part of the ploy to cut off our relationship.

ROSITA: Thanks for the trust. I think we need it before we can deal with this ruthless guy called Augustine.... *(She takes a closer look at his wound.)* You're sure you don't need a doctor?

MARTINS: *(grimaces.)* No. All I need is you. You just do the best you can to take of me...

ROSITA: *(touches him gently.)* You're very hurt, Martins. I'll take you to the hospital...

MARTINS: I say no... I'm fine... Just get me the pain killer in the drawer over there and the first aid box. *(He points to the place.)* You'll take care of me.

ROSITA
Okay... I'll take care of you as you want me to. *(She helps him to lie*

down on the couch before she goes inside one of the rooms.)
ACT FOUR SCENE ONE

(Rosita and Chief Daniel stand at the balcony of his house, facing each other as they talk.)

ROSITA: Nothing can ever make me love Augustine, let alone marrying him. He doesn't have the virtues of a gentleman as you and mum think. He's a mean guy who will get anything he wants by any means. He lacks consideration for others.

CHIEF DANIEL: *(glares at her.)* That's enough!

ROSITA: I'm not done yet, dad.

CHIEF DANIEL: I've heard enough!

ROSITA: Perhaps you should ask why I think he is mean.

CHIEF DANIEL: I don't want to know why. We agreed that you should marry him and you are going to do just that.

ROSITA: Never! Not after he slapped and tried to rape me.

CHIEF DANIEL: What? I don't believe you.

ROSITA: I know you wont believe me but at least I have the right to say "No, I don't" even if you force me to go to the alter with him. Then we'll see who will be at the losing end. *(She snatches her handbag on the chair and hurries out of the sitting room. Chief Daniel looks thoughtful as he walks slowly to couch. He sits down and tales his mobile phone to make a call.)*

CHIEF DANIEL: Hello, Augustine…Yes, how are you…? I'm fine too. Thank you…Yes, I just call to inform you that Rosita just left here. She made a serious allegation against you. Can you come over here when you are chanced and let's talk about it? …All right, see you then. *(He puts down the phone on the centre table, still looking thoughtful.)*

ACT FOUR SCENE TWO

(Augustine and Chief Daniel sit together, talking in the sitting room.)

CHIEF DANIEL: Tell me the truth. Did you hurt and tried to rape her?

AUGUSTINE: *(smiles ruefully.)* You know I can't do a thing like that. How can I rape her? That doesn't make sense, does it? I know she's going to be my wife and I've been waiting to get married to her. How can I possibly do a thing like that, having waited this long?

CHIEF DANIEL: Did you try touching her in any way?

AUGUSTINE: I only tried to kiss her. That's all. I don't know if she considers that as an attempt to rape her.

CHIEF DANIEL: You mean you didn't do any of the things she claimed you did.

AUGUSTINE: None at all. I guess she is involved with another man and she is probably looking for a way to break up with me.

CHIEF DANIEL: That can only happen over my dead body. Are you prepared to marry her right away?

AUGUSTINE: You know I'm ready anytime. Even if you want us to get married tomorrow, I'm ready.

CHIEF DANIEL: I'll talk to her about the wedding. I'm sick and tired of all the fuss she is making about the wedding issue.

AUGUSTINE: I would be delighted if you can get her to marry me soonest.

CHIEF DANIEL: Don't worry. I'll talk to her.

ACT FOUR SCENE THREE

(Augustine is sitting on the couch in his sitting room with Dele and Ramai, drinking)

RAMAI: If you want me to do a neat job for you, I'm taking nothing less than one hundred and fifty thousand naira.

AUGUSTINE: That's a lot of money, baby.

RAMAI: Considering the way I'm going to go about it, it's not. In fact, I may have to come for more if it will involve holding a party.

AUGUSTINE: How are you going to do it?

RAMAI: You don't have to border about that. Leave the shit for the shit man to handle. Leave the mess for me to handle. Yours is to give me all I need and watch me nailing their relationship once and for all. If I'll have to carry his baby and later get rid of it in order to succeed, I'll do it. I'll cling to the guy till you get your woman to the alter.

AUGUSTINE: You sound like a real pro.

RAMAI: I understand the job you want me to do and I'll do it perfectly.

AUGUSTINE: If there is anything you need you*... (He nods at Dele.)* You just let him know. He'll give you everything. You need some cash right away?

RAMAI: Sure.

AUGUSTINE: Hundred thousand enough?

RAMAI: *(nods)* Yep. *(Augustine stands up and goes to his room.)*

ACT FOUR SCENE FOUR

(Chief and Mrs Daniel are with Rosita in her sitting room, talking.)
CHIEF DANIEL: Why are you talking so ill of Augustine now? What

57

has he done to you? *(There is silence as Rosita looks indifferent.)* Tell me, what exactly your problem is?

ROSITA: I don't have any problem. If I have one, it is the mean and ruthless man you want me to marry. You've been listening to him instead of listening to me and that really makes things bad for me.

CHIEF DANIEL: We'll listen to you but first of all tell us if you are keeping a boyfriend. *(Rosita looks reluctant.)* You don't have to hide it from us. Remember we are your parents.

ROSITA: Yes, I have a boyfriend.

MRS DANIEL: *(exchanges glances with Chief Daniel.)* That explains why all our efforts to persuade you to get married to Augustine is proving abortive.

CHIEF DANIEL: Listen, young lady, we, including you have gone far in this issue. In fact, we are at the point of no backing out in the marriage proposal between you and Augustine. So better forget the idea about getting married to someone else because it won't work, no matter what you do.

ROSITA: *(gently appeals to them.)* I don't have to be told that nothing can change your mind but…

CHIEF DANIEL: What are you talking about? We are here to change your mind about the man you are keeping. It won't do you any good. Instead it will bring you a whole lot of problems.

ROSITA: Dad, you are not listening to me. Augustine is the source of my entire problem. Take him out, and I'll have my peace.

MRS DANIEL: What has gotten into you, Rosita?

ROSITA: Nothing, mum. It's my life. I don't need anyone to tell me who I should marry or how to live my life.

CHIEF DANIEL: What are you trying to say now? You mean to tell us we are the ones that influence you to agree to get married to Augustine or what?

ROSITA: I never agree to marry Augustine in the first place. I only agreed to be his girlfriend. That's all.

CHIEF DANIEL: Did you hear yourself? What different does it make? You became his girlfriend so that you can get married, isn't it?

ROSITA: No. I agreed to become his girlfriend until I'm sure if I can tolerate him as a husband. I later discovered that I can't, no matter how I tried. Mum, Dad, I wish you leave me alone and let me live my life the way I like.

CHIEF DANIEL: Don't you think you are missing something here? If you've forgotten what Augustine and his family have done for you and the family, I'll refresh your memory. I'll start by telling you how you acquired this house. You acquired this house through the numerous contracts you got with the connection of Augustine and his family.

ROSITA: That has nothing to do with my refusal to marry him. The contracts came through the relationship between the two families.

CHIEF DANIEL: Did you hear yourself again? You really believe what you said. If you do, you are misleading yourself. It was on the basis that you and Augustine will get married that Augustine and his family have been doing things in our favour, not based on any family relationship. Get that straight into your head.

ROSITA: If that is the reason, we'll reciprocate all he has done.

CHIEF DANIEL: Oh, that's brilliant of you, young lady, but can you tell me how we are going to do that. Tell me how if you think you are smart enough to use another person and dump him like a used tissue paper.

ROSITA: Dad, you know I didn't use him. It was you who had been doing things in my back, making the decisions that are personal to me.

CHIEF DANIEL: *(taps Mrs Daniel and stands up.)* Let's go. We'll see what this will lead her to. *(They leave the sitting room. Rosita who looks upset stands up to go to her room)*

ACT FOUR SCENE FIVE

(Martins is in his office going through some files when the intercom rings. He picks it without dropping the documents.)

MARTINS: Who is she?…Tell her I'm busy… Who send her to me?… Okay, send her in… *(He drops the receiver and continues to study the document. A moment later, Ramai, looking gorgeous enters the office and stands by the door, looking at him expectantly. Martins looks up at her after a while.)*

RAMAI: *(half knells.)* Good afternoon, sir. My name is Ramai Tale.

MARTINS: *(gestures her to the seat in front of him.)* Hello, can I help you?

RAMAI: *(sits down opposite him. She takes out some papers out of her bag.)* Oh, yes. Like you were told on the phone, I'm sent here by Chief Daudu, the Chairman of Daudu group of companies. Actually, he's out of the country right now. *(She brought out a business card and hands it to him. He takes it from her and examines it briefly before he returns it to her.)*

RAMAI: I'm sure you are familiar with him.

MARTINS: Oh, yes. Everybody knows Chief Daudu. We have assisted him to acquire the C of O of his landed property at Victoria Island.

RAMAI: I see, I see. I can see why he directed me to you.

MARTINS: Now I don't have much time. Can you tell me what you want me to do for you, please?

RAMAI: We plan to acquire some landed properties at Maryland and we need the Ministry in the deal. *(She gives him the papers with her. He takes it, looking at it carefully.)*

MARTINS: I don't see what you want us to do here. This is something any estate agent or solicitor can handle.

RAMAI: Well, I'm acting under instructions, sir. I don't know what you want me tell them in the office.

MARTINS: *(picks his complementary card, writes something at the back and hands it over to her.)* The least I can do to help is to direct you to this firm. Tell the manager you come from me. The firm is reputable. It would help you handle the deal.

RAMAI: *(takes the card and the papers from him. She looks at the card and then smiles, looking at him.)* Thank you very much, sir. Can I call you anytime?

MARTINS: Oh, you call me if you have any problem.

RAMAI: *(stands up.)* Once again, thanks for the help, sir.

MARTINS: You are welcome. *(She leaves the room while he resumes to his work.)*

ACT FIVE SCENE ONE

(Martins is in his sitting, watching the television. Rosita is setting the table.)

MARTINS: Better hurry up. I'm starving.

ROSITA: The food is ready. Just give me few more minutes to set the table. *(As she hurries to the kitchen, the telephone rings. Martins goes to pick it up)*

MARTINS: Hello…who am I speaking with?…Ramai? Do I know you?…Oh, I'm sorry, I couldn't remember the name… Did you get what you need from the firm?…. You don't need to thank me that much… Oh yea?…I'm sorry I won't be able to come to your birthday party… I'm sorry to disappoint you…May be next time…Goodbye.

ROSITA: *(places the food on the table, sitting down as Martins comes to join her.)* Who was that?

MARTINS: It's the lady that came to my office sometimes ago, asking me to help her to get an estate agent.

ROSITA: I see *(She serves herself. Martins also serves himself.)* I don't know if I should tell you this

MARTINS: What is it? *(He begins to eat.)*

ROSITA: My parents came to me a few days ago. They tried to persuade me to marry Augustine.

MARTINS: I'm sure they don't know the type of man they want you to marry.

ROSITA: They ask me if I have a boyfriend.

MARTINS: *(looks at her sharply.)* What did you tell them?

ROSITA: What do you expect me to say - deny the fact that I have you?

MARTINS: You think that is save to say.

ROSITA: That's the best time to tell them because I know that sooner or later, they'll get to know. Since Augustine who is the only one posing a serious threat to our relationship is already aware of it, there is there is nothing to hide from anyone again. *(Martins shrugs and continues to eat his food.)*

ACT FIVE SCENE TWO

(Dele and Ramai are in the car that is parked some meters away from Martins' house. They sit beside each other. Dele brings out a bottle of wine and a pack of orange juice. He also takes a syringe with some drug inside. He injects the drug into the pack and empties the content inside the syringe.)

DELE: You've got less than an hour before Rosita shows up.

RAMAI: Yes, I know.

DELE: You must ensure that he drinks out of the orange juice. As you can see, it is the only drink that has the drug.

RAMAI: You don't have to worry. He'll drink it. *(She takes the items and put them in a nylon bag and gets out of the car.)*

DELE: Wait a minute. *(Ramai looks at him through the window of the car.)* Do you have the snacks inside that bag?

RAMAI: Oh, yes, sure. I've got everything I need with me.

DELE: All right then, good luck. I'll see you later. *(He drives away as Ramai goes to Martin's house. The scene changes into Martins' sitting room as he watches the television. Ramai rings the bell. Martins checks his wrist watch before he goes to open the door.)*

RAMAI: *(stands with the nylon bag in her hands.)* Hello, sir!

MARTINS: *(looks a bit surprised to see her.)* Hello…em…What's the name again?

RAMAI: Ramai. You forget names so easily.

MARTINS: What are you doing here?

RAMAI: I've come to see you, of course. I've gone to your office. I was told you've come home.

MARTINS: Sorry for asking so much questions.

RAMAI: It's okay, sir.

MARTHINS: Why are you looking for me?

RAMAI: Oh, I told you I celebrated my birthday last week and I feel the need to celebrate it with you.

MARTINS: That won't be necessary. By the way, how do you where I live?

RAMAI: Everybody in the office knows where you live. Can you please let me in? I have to give you what I have for you.

MARTINS: I'm expecting someone any moment from now. If she sees us together, she may think there is something between us.

RAMAI: Is she your girlfriend?

MARTINS: If you care to know, yes.

RAMAI: She can join us in the celebration. I didn't even know you are still single.

MARTINS: Well, if you don't mind her joining us, come on in then. *(She enters the sitting room. Martins closes the door and gestures her to a seat. He sits opposite her. Ramai brings out the items in the bag.)*

RAMAI: Can I get three cups? When your girlfriend comes, she can join us.

MARTINS: *(He gets the cups in a shelf and gives them to her.)* I wish I know why you find it necessary to spend so much trying to celebrate your birthday with me.

RAMAI: You may not understand but I tell you the help you consider minor is really great and I appreciate it. *(She opens the pack of orange juice.)* I think we should take this juice drink first while waiting for your visitor. When she comes, we'll take the wine. How about that?

MARTINS: *(shrugs.)* It's okay.

RAMAI: *(pours him a full glass while she pours some for herself. She drinks some and gestures him to take his.)* Cheers!

MARTINS: Cheers and happy birthday *(He smiles at her as he drinks some of it.)* I like the taste.

RAMAI: It's the best I can get. *(She drinks some more.)* I have to be careful with this type of drinks. It gives me pile easily.

MARTINS: I see. You're a very lively person.

RAMAI: Thank you, sir. You should have been at the birthday party. It was great.

MARTINS: I'm sorry I couldn't come.

RAMAI: It's okay. *(She pours herself a little more and pour more for Martins)*

MARTINS: That should be okay for me. *(He drinks more. There is a brief silence.)* What do you do at Daudu Group of Companies?

RAMAI: I'm …em….one of their sales rep.

MARTINS: *(looks as if he feels a little dizzy. He puts down the drink.)* Is this drink alcoholic

RAMAI: Not to my knowledge. *(There is another silence before Martins leans on his back and black out.)*

RAMAI: *(sits beside him.)* You can go to your room if you want to sleep.

MARTINS: *(moans.)* Yea, I…

RAMAI: *(helps him on his feet.)* Come on, let me take you to your room. *(She helps him on his feet and practically drags him into one of the bedrooms. She settles him down comfortably on the bed and goes back into the sitting room and scatters the cloths including under wears on the floor. She goes back into the room and begins to remove his shirt and trousers, leaving only his shorts. As she begins to remove her blouse, Rosita drives into the street and packs in front of Martins' house. She winds up the car windows, takes her bag, gets out and locks it. She walks to Martins' house. She presses the doorbell and waits for some times before she opens the door. She looks round and finds the cloths on the floor. Looking puzzled, she picks one of the under wears on the floor. Just then, Ramai speaks from the room.)*

RAMAI: Who is there? *(Rosita goes inside and finds Ramai and Martins on the bed, both are covered with a bed sheet. Ramai is caressing Martins who is deep asleep. She frowns at Rosita.)* What are you doing here?

ROSITA: I should be asking you that question.

RAMAI: What do you mean and who are?

ROSITA: That man you are messing around with is my fiancé.

RAMAI: Your fiancé? You must Rosita Daniel.

ROSITA: Yes. How do you know my name?

RAMAI: *(shrugs.)* He told me about you. *(There is silence as she looks guilty.)* Well, I'm sorry for what you just discovered. I guess I have to explain myself because I don't want to share the consequence of what Martins is trying to do to you. I'm carrying his baby. He has promised to marry me but we need some money to build our home. So... I'm sorry...

ROSITA: That's impossible!

RAMAI: Sssssh, don't wake him up, please. If he gets to know I'm telling you this, I'll be in big trouble. Obviously, I'm not in support of the way he wants to extract money from you. So I'll appreciate it if you keep a secret. *(Rosita begins to leave the room silently.)* Wait for him to wake up. I'll leave now if you don't want me around. *(Rosita looks very disturbed as she gets out of the house slowly. She walks to her car, fumbles with the key, opens the car door with shaking hand, gets inside the car and drives out of the street with top speed.)*

ACT FIVE SCENE THREE

(Chief Daniel is sitting in his car at the back with his driver, driving in the street when his mobile phone begins to ring. He takes the call.)

CHIEF DANIEL: Hello… Yes, I'm Chief Daniel. Who is this?…Yes, she is my daughter… Saint James' Hospital? What's she doing there? …She had an accident? How? When? Where? Is it serious?…I'm on my way now…*(He puts the phone beside him and taps the driver on the shoulder.)* Rosita is in the hospital. She has an accident. You know Saint James hospital at Louis Street?

DRIVER: I know where it is, sir.

CHIEF DANIEL: *(impatiently)* Let's go there now....

(The scene changes to Chief Daniel's car stopping in front of the hospital. He jumps out and hurries into the hospital. He goes to the attendant.) Hello. I'm Chief Daniel. I was told my daughter is here.

ATTENDANT: The lady that had an accident?

CHIEF DANIEL: *(looks impatient.)* Yes, yes.

ATTENDANT: She is in the second room by your left.

CHIEF DANIEL: *(rushes to the room. He opens the door. There are four people in the room, including the doctor and a nurse. He looks at everyone.)* Hello, I'm Chief Daniel…

DOCTOR: You are welcome, Chief.

CHIEF DANIEL: *(goes to Rosita who is lying on the bed with her head bandaged.)* Rosita…

ROSITA: *(whispers.)* Martins…

CHIEF DANIEL: *(looks puzzled.)* Who is Martins?

DOCTOR: *(shrugs.)* We thought you know him.

CHIEF DANIEL: What actually happened?

DOCTOR: *(gestures at Femi.)* This gentleman brought her here. *(He looks at Femi.)* Tell him what happened.

FEMI: I was driving along Mayor Street when she just sped across the junction. It was really a dangerous way to drive. So I drove after her with the hope to stop her but before I can get a way to stop her, she has run into a ditch. I believe that ditch saved her life. If not, with the way she drove, she would have collided with another car that was coming ahead of her. I got her out of the car and brought her here. Since she is able to regain her consciousness, she's been calling the name: Martins. I searched through the items in her car to see if I can find any trace to Martins or someone close to her and I got your number through your complementary card inside.

CHIEF DANIEL: Thank you very much. *(He looks at the doctor.)* Would she be okay?

DOCTOR: She is not seriously wounded. My concern is that she is very hysterical about the person called Martins. I think she must have received a very shocking news about the person. I wish I can see the person and ask him a few questions.

CHIEF DANIEL: But I don't know who Martins is... *(He looks thoughtful.)* Wait, he could be her boyfriend or something.

DOCTOR: Whoever he is, I'll advise you to bring here. Your daughter may be referred to a psychiatric hospital if...

CHIEF DANIEL: *(looks puzzled.)* What? Is it that serious?

DOCTOR: It may not be as serious as that but it is a possibility that she may be referred since we cannot see anything physically wrong with her.

CHIEF DANIEL: I'll call her mother and find out if she knows him. *(He takes his handset and begins to make the call.)* I doubt if she knows him... Hello, I... em...I'm in Saint James Hospital at Louis street.... Rosita had an accident... It's not so serious as I'm told...You can come and see her yourself...wait a minute. I just want to find out if you know any of Rosita's friends called Martins...It's not something we can discuss on the phone but it has to do with her condition...*(He nods vigorously)* ...Do you have her number?...Call her and tell her to join us here at the hospital. It is call Saint James hospital at Louis Street. You know the place?... Tell her Rosita is in the hospital and we need her immediately. If she doesn't know where the hospital is, you can go and pick her while coming. I'll wait for both of you here. *(He looks at the Doctor.)* She doesn't know anyone by that name but she feels my niece may know who he is. My wife will get her here as soon as she can. *(He goes to check Rosita again.)*

ACT FIVE SCENE FOUR

(Martins wakes up on the bed, frowns as he looks round the room. He touches his head and tries to get up. He looks puzzled to find himself without cloths. He puts on his shirt and trousers and goes to the sitting room. Ramai is laying on the couch, drinking some of the wine she has brought. She smiles at Martins who looks surprised to see her.)

MARTINS: What is going on here?

RAMAI: You mean you can't remember?

MARTINS: Remember what...? *(He looks as if he is trying to recall what happened.)*

RAMAI: All right, I'll refresh your memory. I came here to celebrate my birthday with you and you got so drunk that I have to take you to the bed. I removed your cloths. You know, I find you so cute that I couldn't resist you and we did it.

MARTINS: *(frowns.)* We did what?

RAMAI: You really mean you can't remember? We made love.

MARTINS: That's impossible... We were supposed to wait for Rosita to come and... I remember now... It's like you drug me or something.

RAMAI: How could I have drugged you? We both got drunk and went to the room together. *(Just then Nelly parks in front of Martins' house and goes towards the place. She waits as she hears Ramai and Martins, arguing.)*

MARTINS: You cheap prostitute! You drugged me! Why? Tell me what you hope to gain in this.

RAMAI: I told you I love you.

MARTINS: You love me? You must me insane. You think you can win my heart with what you did after telling you I'm involved with a lady.

RAMAI: Have I really done anything wrong?

MARTINS: You mean you don't see what you have done wrong? You came here on the pretense that you are celebrating your birthday; you drugged me and dragged me to bed.

RAMAI: Well, you may not see the point in my way but I have to tell you I'm helplessly in love with you and I feel if you have a taste of me, you'll love me in return.

MARTINS: There is no way I can love a cheap prostitute like you. You are not even descent enough for any man, no matter how wayward he may be. You really want to know how I feel about you. I hate you. I wish you drop dead. I cannot even woo you for my dog.

RAMAI: *(looks angry.)* That's not complementary!

MARTINS: *(points to the door.)* Get out of here! *(Ramai hesitates)* Are you deaf? I said get out of my house. If I see you near my house or office, I'll get you arrested. If you think I can't do that, you just try me. *(As she packs her things, snatching her bag on the floor, Nelly opens the door and enters the sitting room. Ramai leaves, looking angry. Nelly looks at Martins who looks embarrassed.)*

NELLY: Hello, Martins. *(She goes to sit down.)* Who is that lady?

MARTINS: I wish I know where she springs from. She came to my office a few weeks ago and came here today to celebrate her birthday with me. She gave me some juice that made me felt dizzy. Before I knew it, I was on the bed and...

NELLY: I heard all your conversations.

MARTINS: What can I offer you?

NELLY: Nothing. Something serious brought me here.

MARTINS: What is it?

NELLY: Let me ask you if you are expecting Rosita?

MARTINS: Yes, she ought to have been here by now. Did you see her?

NELLY: Yes. I spoke to her before coming here. *(She sighs.)* There is a problem, Martins - a very serious problem.

MARTINS: *(sits down slowly.)* What's wrong?

NELLY: Rosita came here and found that lady who just left.

MARTINS: What?

NELLY: I have a feeling that the lady was set up to ruin your relationship.

MARTINS: That's not a problem. I can go and explain to her.

NELLY: The problem is more complicated than that, Martins. The lady told her she's carrying your baby. She made her believed that you are deceiving her, especially when she found the two of you on the bed together. She said you must have made love together, judging by what she saw. It was with the notion that you've been deceiving her all along that she left this place before she had an accident.

MARTINS: Oh, my God!

NELLY: She kept calling your name in the hospital before I was asked to go and see her in the hospital. I was able to relieve her of what the doctor called hysteria but I couldn't convince her that all the lady told her are lies.

MARTINS: *(looks thoughtful.)* You are right to think this is a set up.

NELLY: I don't know how you are going to do this but you have to come to the hospital and convince her that this is all set up. You don't have to tell me who is behind this. I know but you have to prove this to her. With what I saw and heard, I'll be your witness.

MARTINS: All right. Give me a minute to change.

ACT FIVE SCENE FIVE

(Rosita lies still on the bed while Chief Daniel paces round the room. Mrs Daniel sits on the chair beside Rosita. After a while, there is a gentle knock on the door. Nelly and Martins enter the room. Martins greets them silently with a bow.)

CHIEF DANIEL: Hello, young man. I suppose you are Martins?

MARTINS: Yes, sir.

CHIEF DANIEL: Perhaps you have something to say about what is happening to our daughter.

MARTINS: *(looks as if he is a bit confused.)* I'm not sure you'll like to be around if I try to explain things to her.

CHIEF DANIEL: We've been around since this madness started and we are going to be around until it is over.

NELLY: May be I should first confirm this before he explains himself. I saw the lady Rosita saw with him. I overheard their conversation. She drugged him before she dragged him to the bed. In my candid opinion, I think it is a set up.

ROSITA: *(still closes her eyes.)* I don't believe you, Nelly. *(Everyone looks at her. Martins quickly kneels besides her.)*

MARTINS: Rosita, you've got to believe me. It was a set up. I was waiting for you when the lady came to say she wants to celebrate her birthday with me. I told her I was expecting you. She said you can join us when you return. She gave me a juice drink which is - I don't know. I think it is mixed with drugs. Before I knew it, I was unconscious. That's all I remember before I found the lady still in my sitting room.

ROSITA: *(whispers.)* She said she is carrying your baby.

MARTINS: That's not true. I don't even know her.

CHIEF DANIEL: What are you trying to say? You don't know her but she came to celebrate her birthday with you.

MARTINS: *(He looks at Chief Daniel who is keenly listening to him.)* She came for help in my office which I rendered and she said she wants to show her gratitude by celebrating her birthday with me. *(He looks at Rosita again.)* If you don't believe me, at least, you have to believe your cousin. You think of it. If what you think is true, it would be foolish of me to keep the lady in the house at the time I was expecting you. Believe me, this is a set up? *(There is a long silence. Everyone looks at Rosita who remains still on the bed, still with her eyes closed. Martins stands up in hopeless gesture.)* Rosita, you have the right to believe whatever you can but it's unfair if you don't trust me after all I've gone through because of you.*(He opens the mark on his arm.)* Rosita, look at my hand. Come on, look at it. *(Rosita opens her eyes.)* You treated my arm and my nose when they were bleeding, didn't you?

ROSITA: *(in a whisper.)* Yes.

MARTINS: You remember what you said when I sustained the injury? *(There is silence as he looks hurt.)* I'll remind you. You thanked me for the trust I had in you. You said we'll need it to fight the war. You are supposed to trust me too in front of everybody but you let me down. If there is anything that can make us lose this battle we've been fighting together, it is because you let me down by not trusting me. I wish you well. I'm out of here. *(He turns to go.)*

ROSITA: *(silently.)* Martins, *(He looks at her. Her eyes are full of tears.)* I'm sorry I didn't believe you.

MARTINS: *(whispers.)* It's okay.

ROSITA: *(she stretches her hand at him. Martins looks at Chief Daniels and Mrs Daniel who gesture him to take it. He goes to hold it quietly.)* I love you, Martins.

MARTINS: I love you too. I'll do anything - anything to protect you because you are my life.

ROSITA: Would you do me a favour?

MARTINS: Yes, I'll do anything for you.

ROSITA: Tell my parents what happens to your nose and arm.

MARTINS: *(looks at Chief Daniel briefly before he looks at her.)* I'm sorry I don't think I should do that.

ROSITA: You said you'll do anything for me. So do it for me now. That will prove it to my parents that you are really ready to do anything for me.

MARTINS: Okay. *(He sighs and looks down as he releases her hand.)* Augustine sent some men to beat me up because I'm involved with Rosita. *(Chief Daniel and Mrs Daniel exchanges glances.)*

NELLY: And I think he sets the lady up to ruin their relationship.

ROSITA: *(bursts out sobbing.)* That's the man you want me to marry, dad.

MARTINS: *(holds her hand again.)* It's okay, love. I hate to see you crying.

ROSITA: *(in a whisper.)* Well, I'm formally telling you that Martins is the man I'll marry come what may. Would you accept him as your son in law?

CHIEF DANIEL: You don't mind if we discuss this after you leave this place, do you? *(He looks at Martins.)* Thanks for coming, Martins. I'm sure we'll see again. *(Martins bows, looks at Rosita who smiles at him.)*

NELLY: *(looks at Chief Daniel.)* Uncle, he didn't bring his car. So I have to take him back.

CHIEF DANIEL: It's okay. *(Nelly and Martins go out of the room. They get outside the hospital, talking.)*

NELLY: If there is anything good that came out of this, it is the way you and Rosita proved that you love each other. *(She laughs.)* I wish I could record that scenario. It was like an Indian love movie.

MARTINS: That's not funny, you know. I almost burst out crying when she didn't believe me at the initial stage.

NELLY: That makes it more emotional altogether. The two of you made quite an impact on her parents. Guess what?

MARTINS: What?

NELLY: I felt very proud of the two of you.

MARTINS: I'm no longer a disgrace to you? You gave me that impression at your birthday, remember? *(They laugh as they enter her car and drives out of the hospital premises.)*

ACT SIX SCENE ONE

(Chief Daniel is in his sitting room with Mrs Daniel, sitting opposite each other. Both of them look thoughtful. Mrs Daniel changes her position to sit beside him, looking him.)

MRS DANIEL: We have a problem.

CHIEF DANIEL: *(sighs.)* Yeah, a very big one for that matter.

MRS DANIEL: What are we going to do about it?

CHIEF DANIEL: I've been thinking of it. Up till now I don't know what we have to do.

MRS DANIEL: Obviously, Augustine should not be considered for marriage with Rosita again if we mean well for her.

CHIEF DANIEL: Yes. It's hard to believe that Augustine is as mean as that.

MRS DANIEL: Yes, it's hard. I think we should just call his family and let them know what we feel now.

CHIEF DANIEL: That would be very difficult. Apart from what happened at the hospital, we have no proof of what we know. Dr Cole may feel we just decided to support Rosita because we could not bring her to marry his son.

MRS DANIEL: Do we have to care about what anybody feels, considering the happiness of our only daughter?

CHIEF DANIEL: It's more than that, you know. The situation is like the business Augustine and his family have invested in and they expect dividend from it. Changing our minds about it is like breaching a contract.

MRS DANIEL: Then let's breach it. We can't afford to trade with the joy of our daughter.

CHIEF DANIEL: You are right but there is way we have to go about it.

MRS DANIEL: I don't care how we do it. We must support Rosita in getting married to the man of her choice.

CHIEF DANIEL: We'll tell Rosita to get married to the man secretly.

MRS DANIEL: Why?

CHIEF DANIEL: That seems to be the only way out. No matter what happens now, we must not give Augustine and his family the impression that we know anything about her involvement with another man.

MRS DANIEL: *(looks thoughtful.)* How do we convince our relations and friends that we don't know anything about the marriage?

CHIEF DANIEL: We simply go out of the town on official duty at the time they'll get married.

MRS DANIEL: We can't do that!

CHIEF DANIEL: I'm afraid that is what we have to do. That's the price we must pay.

MRS DANIEL: Then what happens when they get married? I'm sure you expect some reactions. How do you handle that?

CHIEF DANIEL: That's easier to handle than to go and face the family, telling them that Rosita can longer marry Augustine. At least, after the marriage, we'll let them see that we did all we could get her to marry Augustine. At that point, we can request the family to tell us what we should do to pay back what they have invested in the proposed marriage. After all, the law does not make it mandatory that parents must support the marriage between two people. So there is little we can do to stop them.

MRS DANIEL: What if they get to know we know about the marriage after all? Besides, we are not sure if Rosita and her boyfriend will buy that idea.

CHIEF DANIEL: I'm sure they would, judging by what I noticed between the two of them. I don't see how people will know we are aware of the secret marriage if we tell no one.

MRS DANIEL: Well... *(The telephone rings. She goes to pick it.)* Hello... Oh, Augustine, how are you...? *(She looks at Chief Daniel who quickly shakes his head, waving and indicating that he does not want to talk to him.)* He just went out now... Oh, I thought you know what happened to her. She had an accident yesterday while coming from the office... It's not serious at all. In fact, she is at home now... Okay then. *(She puts down the phone. She looks at Chief Daniel who still looks thoughtful.)* Did I sound friendly enough? *(Chief Daniel shrugs.)*

ACT SIX SCENE TWO

(Dele and Ramai are in a room, sitting together on the couch.)

DELE: I'm sure Augustine would be impressed by the job you have done so far.

RAMAI: I hope so.

DELE: Did you actually sleep with the guy?

RAMAI: What's your concern about that?

DELE: Hay, you can not say if I am interested.

RAMAI: You think I jump into bed with any man?

DELE: Can you jump into the bed with me?

RAMAI: No.

DELE: Why not?

RAMAI: You need to be tested of HIV first. A man like you must have gone to bed with many women.

DELE: *(He laughs.)* You see yourself as a saint, don't you? *(The doorbell rings.)* That must be Augustine. *(He goes to open the door. Augustine smiles at him as he enters.)* You are so quick. *(He closes the door and follows him.)*

AUGUSTINE: I didn't spend much time with her. *(He sits down opposite Ramai, smiling at her.)* You shouldn't have given my lady a shock like that. It almost cost her her life. She had an accident while thinking of what you must have told her.

RAMAI: You wouldn't blame me for that, would you?

AUGUSTINE: I'm not blaming you really. I just want to inform you that the effect was great. I don't think I want you to give her a shock like that again. I believe with what you have told her so far, we should be on our way to get married. *(He brings out an envelope and* *throws it to her.)* That's hundred thousand naira for you. The deal is over.

RAMAI: *(looks inside the envelope.)* Thanks! *(She looks at him.)* What if the guy tries to stage a come back?

AUGUSTINE: I don't think he'll succeed if he tries to. If it looks as if he will, we'll call on you.

RAMAI: *(stands up)* All right. I'm available anytime.

DELE: How about my offer, sweetheart?

RAMAI: You can write me an application letter. I'll consider it. *(She looks at Augustine.)* Thanks.

AUGUSTINE: You are welcome. *(Ramai leaves the room.)*

ACT SIX SCENE THREE

(Rosita lies on the couch, talking on the phone; laughing whole heartedly.)

ROSITA: …Martins, I'm not in the mood for those cracks. Save them till another time… He was here. He was trying to get some information about the effect of what he tried to do… Well, I gave him the impression that I don't trust any man including him… Of course, that gave him the idea that he has succeeded in breaking our relationship. He didn't know he only makes things worse for himself. For now, we need to give him the impression that my relationship with you is over and let me parents come up with what to do… Of course, they are on our side now… *(The house maid leads Chief Daniel into the sitting room. She stands up as soon as she sees him.)*

HOUSE MAID: *(Silently.)* Can I get you anything, sir?

CHIEF DANIEL: *(goes to sit down)* No, thanks. *(The house maid leaves.)*

ROSITA: Hold on a moment. My father is here… *(She smiles at Chief Daniel.)* It's Martins.

CHIEF DANIEL: Say my greetings to him.

ROSITA: *(talks into the phone again.)* Dad says "hi"… Okay then… Bye, I love you too… *(She laughs.)* I'm going to tell him what you just said now. *(She laughs again.)* Okay, I'll not tell him. Would that give you a good night sleep…? Okay... Bye. *(She puts the phone down on the table and looks at Chief Daniel.)*

CHIEF DANIEL: What did he say which he doesn't want me to know?

ROSITA: I promised him I'll not tell you.

CHIEF DANIEL: I'm just curious.

ROSITA: He said I shouldn't tell him I love him in your presence. He

73

said it makes him feel uncomfortable if I said that in your presence.

CHIEF DANIEL: I see. Well, I'm here to talk about you and Augustine. *(There is a brief silence.)* It is clear to us now that he is not the kind of man we should desire for you but we don't want him or his family to know that we support your marriage with another man.

ROSITA: Why?

CHIEF DANIEL: You don't have to ask me why. You already know the reason.

ROSITA: How can we get married without people knowing that you support us?

CHIEF DANIEL: You already have our support. It doesn't have to be given in the open. So talk to Martins that your mother and I want you to get married in secret. When you are about to do that, we'll go to Abuja.

ROSITA: *(frowns.)* Why do we have to do it that way, dad?

CHIEF DANIEL: That is the only way we can convince Augustine and his family that we never intended you for another man. Besides that's the only way we can be justified if we offer to pay all they might have invested in your marriage proposal with him.

ROSITA: I can't see that as a good reason we should do it secretly. What stops us from telling them that I'm not interested in marrying Augustine again and we are ready to pay everything they think they have invested in the proposal? After all, the issue of marriage is not business issue.

CHIEF DANIEL: That's exactly the point. I just realize that Augustine sees his marriage with you as a business issue. Going by the way he's fighting so hard to marry you, I have no doubt that he's planning to expand his business empire through the marriage. The only way you can prove that you are not a business he can invest on is to go straight to the registry and get married as secretly as possible. I can use that as the basis to return all they have invested so far and tell them your marriage is not a business. Once the law recognizes that you are married, nobody not even any of your parents can contest it. That is the reason the registry is often given at least twenty-one days notice before people can be joined as husband and wife. If anyone has any reason the marriage should not be instituted, he or she is expected to enter what they call a caveat within that period. Let me tell you something important about marriage. Real marriage is not the noise people make during celebration but something that start from the day you actually start living together as husband and wife. From what I notice in your relationship with Martins, you have all the ingredients that can make your marriage a huge success. So do all you can to persuade him to marry you secretly as soon as possible.

ROSITA: *(smiles at him.)* I don't need to persuade him, dad. He will do it if he knows it's going to make me happy.

CHIEF DANIEL: *(returns the smiles.)* I must confess that I like your Martins.

ROSITA: Thanks, dad. Can I tell him?

CHIEF DANIEL: No, not yet. *(He stands up.)* I have to go now. You need feed me back after you have talked with him about it. *(Rosita follows him as he leaves the room.)*

ACT SIX SCENE FOUR

(Nelly is reading a magazine in her sitting when the doorbell rings. She goes to open the door. Martins stands in front of her.)

NELLY: *(smiles.)* Hello, secret lover.

MARTINS: *(enters the sitting room.)* If you think it's proper to laugh at me, fine.

NELLY: *(follows him, singing.)* Secret lovers, that's what you are…

MARTINS: Nelly, I don't think that's funny.

NELLY: You don't have to sound so serious.

MARTINS: Do you know how it feels to leave my home and Rosita's and come here to see her just because we have to keep our affairs a secret?

NELLY: What's wrong in meeting here? After all, you met her here and you woo her here. *(Rosita drives to the front of Nelly's house. She gets out, winds the glass and goes to press the doorbell. Nelly opens the door and smiles at her)* Hello, big cousin.

ROSITA: *(smiles and hugs her.)* Hi. *(They go to join Martins after Nelly has closed the door. She goes to kiss Martins on the cheek. He smiles at her.)* You've been here for long?

MARTINS: *(pretends to look offended.)* Long enough to hear your cousin singing song about secret lovers.

ROSITA: *(laughs loudly, looking at Nelly who also laugh.)* How dare you treat my love like that, Nelly! *(She sits beside Martins.)* You don't have to mind her. She's just jealous.

NELLY: Why should I be jealous of you? I have my boyfriend too.

MARTINS: I should have known you are truly jealous. You are jealous because your affair with your boyfriend is a long distance affair. Ours may be secret love, at least, we see each other as long as we want. God knows when you'll see yours.

NELLY: You don' have to worry about that. In due course, I'll be out of Nigeria to join him.

MARTINS: You can get out if you like. The country is too small for the two of us anyway. *(The rest laugh.)*

ROSITA: *(looks at Martins.)* On a serious note, my father wants me to have a serious discussion with you.

MARTINS: I'm sure it's about us.

ROSITA: Off course, yes.

NELLY: You wouldn't mind if I leave the two of you alone?

ROSITA: I want you to be around. That's the reason I'm saying this now.

NELLY: Let me get you something to drink first. *(She goes inside the kitchen to get some drinks.)*

ROSITA: You wouldn't believe it if I tell you what my father wants me to discuss with you.

MARTINS: I'm sure it's about our relationship.

ROSITA: It's more than that. Can you make a guess?

MARTINS: No. Please, tell me and don't put me in suspense. *(Nelly brings the drinks, hands a glass to each of the and sits opposite them, sipping hers.)*

ROSITA: Nelly, you won't believe it. My father told me to get married secretly to Martins.

MARTINS: *(looks at Nelly who merely shrugs.)* If that's a joke, it's quite expensive, you know.

ROSITA: I'm serious. He told me this yesterday, the time we were talking on the phone. In fact, he wants me to inform him what we decide as soon as possible.

MARTINS: Why did he want us to do that?

ROSITA: He feels that's the only way he can convince Augustine and his family that he didn't intend me to marry another man.

MARTINS: That implies that he would not be at the wedding?

ROSITA: He won't. In fact, he would be at Abuja with my mother.

MARTINS: I wish I understand why we have to…

NELLY: What else do you have to understand, Martins?

MARTINS: It's strange, you know.

NELLY: What's strange about that? You need her, you got her. Now is the time to get what you want in whichever way can.

MARTINS: It looks like an easy way out, you know.

NELLY: You want a tough way out of this, no problem. Go and tell Augustine to his face that you want to marry his fiancée. Then he'll show you the real tough way. *(The rest laugh.)*

ROSITA: *(holds Martins hand.)* Actually, Martins, I didn't like the idea at first. You know, I dream of big society wedding where this guy, Sunny Nneji will come and sing at the reception like this *(She sings and moves sideways. Nelly sings with her.)* Oruka ti d'owo na. Di ololufere mu. Ko seni tole ya yin titi lai… But, you see, my father said something I'll never forget. He said real marriage is not the noise we make out of it. It is the actual living together as a husband and wife in peace and harmony that is called marriage.

MARTINS: *(nods.)* That was very sound. We'll do it.

ROSITA: We'll go and fill the form at the registry right away.

MARTINS: Yeah, right away if that's what you want.

ROSITA: *(hugs him)* Oh, I love you so much.

MARTINS: *(looks at Nelly who looks away.)* Somebody is really jealous here. *(They all laugh.)*

ACT SIX SCENE FIVE

(Augustine sits opposite Chief Daniel and Mrs Daniel in Chief Daniel's sitting room, talking.)

CHIEF DANIEL: You see the issue of marriage cannot come up now because, as you know, I'm still trying to persuade Rosita. She is proving very stubborn but I can assure you that she would listen to me sooner or later. She is already cooling down the last time I talk about it with her. She wants me to give her more time. So you have to be more patient. I can understand that you have waited a long time but like our people normally say, patience can cook a stone. I'm sure you know what that implies.

AUGUSTINE: Yes, sir. I understand it and I'm glad you encourage me in the relationship. Actually, I thought Rosita was involved with another man. I'm not sure if you confirm this from her.

CHIEF DANIEL: She confessed it to me at the hospital but something happened which made her change her mind about the guy. She didn't tell me what happened but I guess the guy jilted her or something. That was what gave me a better chance to talk more about you. I don't want to border her because I know she would soon come back to her senses.

AUGUSTINE: That's good news to me, sir.

MRS DANIEL: You can keep hoping for the best.

AUGUSTINE: Thank you, ma. *(He looks at Chief Daniel.)* And thank you too, sir. I quite appreciate all your efforts.

CHIEF DANIEL: It's a pleasure. After all, every good parent would love to have a gentleman like you for a son-in-law?

AUGUSTINE: *(smiles as he stands up.)* I'm flattered, sir.

CHIEF DANIEL: It's the truth.

AUGUSTINE: Thank you for the complement then. I hope to see you some other time.

CHIEF DANIEL: *(stands up to see him off.)* Before I forget I have to inform you that my wife and I are invited to Abuja to attend a week seminar by a one of my colleagues. It will be starting next week. So we'll be going on Sunday. Tell your father I won't be able to attend the chapter meeting of the association that is scheduled for next week. I'll get all the information about the meeting from him when I return.

AUGUSTINE: I'll tell him. I wish you success in your journey if we don't see before then. *(He addresses Mrs Daniel.)* Goodbye, ma.

MRS DANIEL: Good bye, my son.

CHIEF DANIEL: Thanks a lot for coming. *(He follows Augustine who opens the door that leads outside the house. He closes it as Chief Daniel returns to his seat. Augustine gets into his car outside and drives away.)*

MRS DANIEL: *(looks at Chief Daniel.)* Who would imagine a man like that can be violent enough to beat up another man because of a lady?

CHIEF DANIEL: Do you notice the way he's trying to find out if Rosita and Martins have reconciled?

MRS DANIEL: I noticed it.

CHIEF DANIEL: Before he knows what is about to strike him, he would have been knocked out with surprise.

MRS DANIEL: I hope Rosita and Martins would get married on the day they have chosen.

CHIEF DANIEL: Rosita told me everything is order. Only six people would be at the registry with the couple. Nelly is one of them. Martins' parents and three other people will witness the marriage. There will be more people that will celebrate it at Martins residence.

MRS DANIEL: Looks as if they have put so many things in order.

CHIEF DANIEL: Both of them are smart very smart.

ACT SEVEN SCENE ONE

(Dele looks impatient as he paces up and down in Augustine's sitting room. A moment later, Augustine comes into the sitting room. He hurries to him.)
AUGUSTINE: What seems to be the problem?
DELE: There is something you really need to come and see at the house of Rosita's boyfriend.
AUGUSTINE: *(looks anxious.)* What's happening there?
DELE: Are you sure you are prepared for this shock?
AUGUSTINE: Tell me what it is.
DELE: I think you better come and see it yourself. I won't be the one to tell you.
AUGUSTINE: Let's go. *(They leave the room immediately.)*

ACT SEVEN SCENE TWO

(There is a party at Martins' house. Music plays as there is celebration. Rosita who is in a wedding gown goes round the people with Martins who is in black suit, holding hands. People are congratulating them. Dele and Augustine park outside the compound, looking at the people inside.)
AUGUSTINE: What's going on here?
DELE: I don't know what you call it. But what I think we have here is wedding celebration.
AUGUSTINE: This is impossible!
DELE: I didn't believe it when I saw it
AUGUSTINE: *(looks at Rosita and Martins as they greet the people.)* That guy is a dead man. Let's go, man. *(The car drives away.)*

ACT SIX SCENE THREE

(Martins and Rosita are sitting together on the couch with her head lying against his chest.)
MARTINS: I can't believe I'm married.
ROSITA: *(laughs.)* Perhaps you'll believe it when I'm heavy with twins.
MARTINS: Twins! You must be kidding.
ROSITA: *(laughs.)* What's wrong in having twins?
MARTINS: Nursing a baby is burdensome, let alone twins.
ROSITA: If I give birth to twins, what would you do? Run out of the

house?

MARTINS: We'll give one of them to your mother and keep the one we can take care. *(Rosita laughs again. Just then the doorbell rings.)* Who is it?

EVANGELIST: *(from outside.)* It's me evangelist Sola.

MARTINS: *(stands up to go and open the door.)* Hello, can we help you?

EVANGELIST: Good afternoon.

MARTINS: Good afternoon.

EVANGELIST: I have a message for you from the Lord.

MARTINS: From who?

EVANGELIST: The Lord Jesus. Can you, please, let me in? *(Martins opens the door.)*

EVANGELIST: Are you the man who just married few days ago?

MARTINS: Yes. Is there any problem?

EVANGELIST: The Lord sent me to you and your wife.

ROSITA: Martins, let him come and sit down.

MARTINS: *(gestures him to a seat.)* Have your seat.

EVANGELIST: *(goes to face Rosita as Martins follows him.)* I don't need to sit because the message may cause you to kick me out of this house.

ROSITA: Why should we do that? You are a man of God, I suppose.

EVANGELIST: Yes, I'm a man of God but sometimes the message of a man of God can be so unpleasant for people to bear. I'm not sure if you will be able to bear this.

MARTINS: *(goes to sit beside Rosita.)* Tell us, all the same.

EVANGELIST: *(paces in front of them.)* Before I tell you what the Lord wants me to tell you, let me tell you the fact that your life is full of complications because both of you are sinners. It's going to get much more complicated if you continue in sin.

MARTINS: Why calling us sinners? Did we steal anything?

EVANGELIST: *(smiles)* Stealing is not the only sin in the world. Besides I didn't call you sinners. The Bible says you are sinners in the book of Romans chapter 3 verse 23. The passage says that all have sinned and fallen short of the glory of God. *(He takes a pocket Bible in his breast pocket, opens it and begins to read.)* Aagain, according to the book of Galatians chapter five verses nineteen to twenty-one, sin is any attributes of the flesh such as adultery, fornication, uncleanness, lasciviousness, idolatry, witchcraft, hatred, variance, emulations, wrath, strife, seditions, heresies, envyings, murder, drunkenness, revelings and such like.

80

The Bible goes on to say in verse twenty-one that anyone who is involved in any of these will not inherit the kingdom of God. You cannot claim not to have done any of these, can you?

ROSITA: *(looks at Martins who also looks at her before she looks back at Evangelist.)* We've committed a good number of what you just read.

EVANGELIST: So you agree with me now that you are both sinners, don't you?

ROSITA: *(silently)* Yes.

EVANGELIST: *(looks at Matins.)* How about you?

MARTINS: Yes, we are sinners.

EVANGELIST: That makes my mission here very easy. The next question is do you want to continue in sin and expose yourself to both physical and eternal deaths?

ROSITA AND MARTINS: *(At the same time)* No.

EVANGELIST: I suppose you want to get out of your sin?

ROSITA AND MARTINS: Yes.

EVANGELIST: Then there is hope for you. I'll read the word of God to you again in the Gospel according to Saint John chapter one verse twelve. It says, "but as many as receive him - that's Jesus Christ - to them he gave the power to become children of God, even to them that believes in his name." *(He looks at them briefly. They are very attentive.)* After becoming children of God, you can then look at your enemies in the face and declare what the Bible says in the first Epistle of John chapter four verse four. *(He turns the Bible to the page)* It says, "You are of God, little children, and have overcome them: because greater is he that is in you, than he that is in the world." *(He looks at them)* Isn't that wonderful? But without Christ, nothing can ever be right in your life. Without Jesus Christ reigning in your lives, you would not have the right to sleep with your two eyes closed, you'll not have any peace. A life outside Christ is a life of crisis and second death in a place called hell. *(He begins to pace again.)* I think I can now tell you what the Lord asked me to tell you. According to the message, you have offended someone with your marriage. That person will stop at nothing until... *(He points at Martins.)* he sees you dead! *(Martins and Rosita look stunned as they exchange glances.)* I don't know who that person is but he is after your life as we talk now.

ROSITA: *(looks impatient.)* Will he succeed getting his life, sir?

EVANGELIST: That depends on him. If you draw close to God, there is no way he can get at you. You don't need anyone to tell you that anyone who is far away from his maker is dinning with the devil with a very short spoon.

ROSITA: Where is your church, sir? We'll like to be coming there.

EVANGELIST: I'm not here to preach about church to you but to tell you of the need to have a personal relationship with Jesus Christ.

MARTINS: All the same we need a place where we can be taught more about the word of God.

EVANGELIST: *(gives Martins the pocket Bible.)* You can have this. That's all you need to survive. Read it, do what it says and take it with you wherever you go. God will protect and be with you if do. As for where to worship God, ask God to lead you to a living church. It is not every church you see that is with God. In fact some are established by the devil to deceive people.

ROSITA: We'll like to be coming to your church, sir, if you don't mind.

EVANGELIST: *(takes a card from his pocket and gives it to Rosita who quickly takes it and looks at it with Martins.)* That is the address of my church with my phone number. Feel free to call anytime and more importantly, you must pray hard.

MARTINS: Can you pray for us now, sir?

EVANGELIST: Let's start by asking you to confess all your sins to God. Promise him that you will never go back to them. *(Martins and Rosita kneel down in front of Evangelist and begin to pray with their eyes closed.)*

ACT SIX SCENE FOUR

(Martins and Rosita just finish shopping. They get out of the supermarket with bags of items and walk to the main road.)

MARTINS: You can stay here while I get the car. *(He puts down the bags beside Rosita who puts down the ones she is holding.)*

ROSITA: All right. *(Martins moves towards the road, looking his left and right sides.)* Be careful. *(As Martins crosses the road, a car suddenly appears at top speed. Rosita screams hysterically, covering her mouth with both hands.)* Martins! (Martins dives across the road. The car misses narrowly. The car drives away without stopping. Martins sits beside the road, looking at the car. A stranger comes to help him on his feet.)*

STRANGER: That was close. Are you okay?

MARTINS: *(takes out the small Bible in his pocket.)* Yeah, I think so.

STRANGER: I can see that you are Christian.

MARTINS: Yea, I just became real one.

STRANGER: *(pats him on the shoulder.)* Take my advice: stick to your God. There is no way you could have survived if that car hit you.

MARTINS: *(looks at Rosita running across the road, moving towards him.)* Yea. Thanks. *(The stranger goes away)*

ROSITA: *(runs into his arms, crying.)* Oh, Martins!

MARTINS: It's okay, honey. I'm okay. That's a proof that God is with us.

ACT SIX SCENE FOUR

(Augustine sits in his compound, looking furious as three men stand in front of him in his house.)

AUGUSTINE: How could you possibly miss? *(He stands up to look round at them.)* You guys are the clumsiest creatures I have ever known. You have been watching this guy for days, looking for the opportunity to hit him. When you had the chance, you blew it!

FIRST MAN: Give us another chance, boss.

AUGUSTINE: You want another chance? Do you know what it means for you to lose the first chance? You just gave that guy the signal that his life is in danger. Besides that, the woman would guess who is behind this.

SECOND MAN: We'll watch over his house every night until we are able to hit him. We'll cart away all his valuables and make it appear as if he's knocked off by armed robbers.

AUGUSTINE: *(looks thoughtful for a while.)* What if the lady is with him as usual?

SECOND MAN: We'll still first ask him of the money he collects in the bank in the presence of the lady. If he claims not to have all the money we ask from him, we'll waste him. That's the best way to make it appear as armed robbery.

AUGUSTINE: Do you have any gun to use for that operation?

THIRD MAN: That's not a problem. We know where to get a gun.

AUGUSTINE: All right. I'll give you the chance to hit him again and make it appear like robbery. If for any reason the lady is not around, you can raid the house.

SECOND MAN: That shouldn't be difficult to do.

AUGUSTINE: Now, listen: If you blow the chance again, you are doomed.

THIRD MAN: We'll not fail this time. No matter what it takes, we'll see to it that the guy is dead.

AUGUSTINE: You can go and don't come back here without wasting the guy. You understand?

ALL THE MEN: Yes, sir. *(They leave the room.)*

ACT SIX SCENE FIVE

(Martins is putting on his shirt in Rosita's room while she sits on the bed, looking at him.)

ROSITA: Why don't you sleep with me here tonight? We'll go and sleep down there tomorrow?

MARTINS: I told you there's a file I have to work on at home before tomorrow morning. I forgot it there. If not, I would have stayed overnight.

ROSITA: Can I go with you then?

MARTINS: What is the use? I'm going there to work. So we may not have much time. *(He smiles at her as she sighs.)* I promise you I'll have more than enough time for you tomorrow.

ROSITA: *(shrugs.)* All right.

MARTINS: *(puts on his coat and kisses her on the cheek, standing up.)* I'll see you tomorrow.

ROSITA: Good night, love.

MARTINS: Good night. *(He goes towards the door.)*

ROSITA: *(As she leans backward, her hand touches the pocket Bible on the bed.)* Martins. *(He looks at her.)* You forgot the Bible.

MARTINS: *(goes to take it from her, smiling at her.)* Thanks. *(He puts it in the breast pocket of his coat before he goes out, blowing kisses at her.)*

ACT SIX SCENE SIX

(The three men are in the car in front of Martins' house at night.)

FIRST MAN: *(sits behind the wheel and looks at the other two.)* I'm not sure this guy is coming here tonight.

SECOND MAN: He comes home everyday. There is no time he stays outside since we've been watching over him.

THIRD MAN: What if the lady persuades him to stay with her for tonight?

SECOND MAN: We'll try again tomorrow until we are able to perform our job.

FIRST MAN: I'm beginning to find this very boring.

THIRD MAN: You don't have to. You were the one that missed the first chance to hit the guy.

FIRST MAN: Are you blaming me for that? After all you had the chance to hit him too.

SECOND MAN: What's the point in this? We missed the chance, we missed together. Blaming anyone does not fix the problem. *(Martins drives into the street and turns towards his premises. Second man points at him.)* That's him now. He's all alone.

THIRD MAN: We don't have to border how to handle the lady. Let's give him a few minutes to get in. *(He brings out a gun.)* I'll knock him off straight away. The two of you can get ready to find anything valuable in the house.

ACT SEVEN SCENE ONE

(Martins enters the sitting room, switches the light on and closes the door. He goes into his room, switching on the light. He goes to take the files on the table, looking through them. Suddenly, the door bursts open and the third man puts a gun at him. He smiles wickedly at him. Martins holds his hands up.)

MARTINS: What do you want?

THIRD MAN: We've come to end your miserable life. We've been watching you for days now. Man, you are lucky we couldn't hit you with the car. This time, you are a rotten corpse. Say your last prayer.

MARTINS: *(closes his eyes. His lips trembles in a whisper.)* Have mercy on me oh Lord... *(There is a flash back of the Evangelist saying, "God will protect and be with you if do...")* Lord, remember your promise to be with me... *(He is still closing his eyes when the gun is shot at him. He falls backward on the bed. The third man smiles and then turns away to go, closing the door. After a while, Martins opens his eyes, looking surprised. He feels his chest and touches the Bible. He quickly brings it out. The bullet is stuck in the Bible. He holds it tightly and closes his eyes tightly and opens them. He quickly takes the phone in his other pocket and begins to make a call.)*

ACT SEVEN SCENE TWO

(Rosita is reading the Bible on the bed when her phone rings beside her. She looks at it and smiles. She receives the call.)

ROSITA: Hello, love... *(She looks agitated.)* What! I'll call the police... *(She jumps out of the bed. She is in night gown. She wraps herself with a wrapper on the bed and dashes out of the room, pressing some numbers in her phone with trembling hand as she hurries out.)*

ACT SEVEN SCENE THREE

(The three men are taking some items out of Martins' house. After a while, Rosita's car and a police car drive into the street. The two cars are packed some meters away from Martins' house. Five policemen come out of the cars. Holding a gun each, they

sneak into Martins' house. A policeman sits beside Rosita who looks impatient.)

FIRST POLICE MAN: *(looks at the other men.)* I think the men are still inside the house.

ROSITA: *(impatiently.)* That would be very dangerous for my husband.

FIRST POLICE MAN: There's nothing to worry about. My men would handle them. *(He looks at the other police men again. Three of them move round the house while the other two get ready to enter the door that is still opened. The three men are still in the sitting room, looking around for what they will take. The police men burst in, pointing their guns at them.)*

SECOND POLICE MAN: Freeze or we'll shoot! *(The men look stunned as they raise up their hands.)* Where are the rest?

THIRD MAN: *(still having the gun in his hand.)* It's just three of us.

SECOND POLICE MAN: *(goes to snatch the gun from third man. He nods at his partner.)* You take them away. I'll check the rooms. *(His partner urges the three men out with his gun while the second policeman goes to check inside each room, pointing his gun at every direction he faces. He gets to the room where Martins is still pretending to be dead. The second policeman moves slowly to him, touching him gently.)* Hello. Are you okay?

MARTINS: *(opens his eyes.)* Yea, I think I'm okay.

SECOND POLICE MAN: Your wife is waiting in the car. *(They leave the room. Rosita and the other policemen that are waiting outside with the three men. Rosita runs to embrace Martins. The three men are ushered into their own car with two of the policemen by their sides.)*

FIRST POLICE MAN: *(goes to join Martins and Rosita.)* Well, sir. You'll have to come to the station with us. We'll need your statement.

MARTINS: All right. Thanks for the rescue.

FIRST POLICE MAN: You don't have to. It's our job. *(He beckons on the other policemen to join him in the car.)* Let's go, boys. *(Martins quickly goes to lock the door of his house before he joins them in the car.)*

ACT SEVEN SCENE FOUR

(Chief Daniel and Mrs Daniel are sitting at the back of their car as the driver drives them into the premises. It packs in front of the

87

entrance. Chief Daniel and Mrs Daniel get down from the car. Just then, Chief Daniels' phone begins to ring. He takes it out of his pocket receives the call.)

CHIEF DANIEL: Hello, Dr Cole…yea…I'm just returning. In fact we have not yet entered the house… What's wrong? …What? What did he do? …I'll be expecting you. *(He looks thoughtful as he put the phone back in his pocket.)*

MRS DANIEL: What is wrong?

CHIEF DANIEL: I was told that Augustine had been arrested. His father said he's been trying to reach me since. He said he needs my help.

MRS DANIEL: What has Augustine done this time?

CHIEF DANIEL: He's coming to tell us. I'm almost sure it has to do with Rosita. *(He and Mrs Daniel walk to the entrance as the driver takes their luggage out the car.)*

ACT SEVEN SCENE FIVE

(Evangelist sits opposite Martins and Rosita who sit beside each other on the couch in Martins' sitting room)

MARTINS: … If not for that Bible, I would have been a dead man by now. The bullet stuck right into the Bible. The hired killer thought I was dead. That was the second attempt the people made to terminate my life.

EVANGELIST: How do you know they are the same people that made the first attempt?

MARTINS: The killer confirmed it before he shot at me.

EVANGELIST: I'm sure this is over now.

ROSITA: *(holds Martins' hand, smiling.)* It is. The people involved are now in police custody.

MARTINS: They are trying to use their powerful connections to get out of it but I'm using my office to ensure that they don't get away with it.

EVANGELIST: *(smiles at him.)* I'm sure you are not trying to take revenge.

MARTINS: No, no, sir. I just want the law to take its course. That's all. Besides, that's the only way to feel secured.

EVANGELIST: Only God can secure your life.

MARTINS: I know that, sir. In fact, my faith in God is so much that I can trust him with everything about my life.

EVANGELIST: *(stands up.)* That's what you need before you can walk with God. I have to go now. *(The other two also stand to see* *him off.)* I hope to see you in the church on Sunday.

MARTINS: We'll be around as usual. We can't do without God.

EVANGELIST: I'm glad to hear that. *(He looks at them.)* The two of you must begin to think of the service you will render to the Lord for what he has done for you.

ROSITA: Really, I'm thinking of joining the choir.

EVANGELIST: *(looks at Martins.)* How about you?

MARTINS: I don't know yet. You can tell me what you want me to do.

EVANGELIST: You can join the men's group.

MARTINS: I'll do that. *(He opens the door for him.)*

ACT SEVEN SCENE SIX

(Chief Daniel looks keenly at Dr Cole and Mrs Cole while Mrs Daniel looks surprised.)

CHIEF DANIEL: Did you say Rosita is married?

DR COLE: Yes, but that is not the main problem.

CHIEF DANIEL: To you, that may not be the problem. It is a big problem for my only daughter to get married just like that, especially to the man I don't know.

DR COLE: *(looks regretful.)* I wish I can explain better than this but I can't. Three robbers attempted to kill the man that married Rosita. They were caught and tortured. They said my son sent them just because the men worked with him.

CHIEF DANIEL: *(takes his phone.)* I'm confused about this. I'll call Rosita here. Perhaps she can explain what exactly is going on.

MRS COLE: You can tell her to bring the man here too.

CHIEF DANIEL: Why should I do that? I'm not sure I believe what you are saying about her marriage with a man I don't know.

DR COLE: She can bring him all the same.

CHIEF DANIEL: *(talks into the phone)* …Hello, Rosita... I just return few hours ago. Now listen. Dr Cole is here with me now. He's saying something I don't understand. He said you are married. I don't believe him anyway. Perhaps you can come down here with the man you married and explain what is happening… Make it snappy… *(He put down the phone and looks at the rest.)* She is on her way.

MRS DANIEL: What I don't understand is the link between the robbery and Augustine.

MRS COLE: According to what he told us, it is because the men work with him…

MRS DANIEL: *(interupts her)* How come about robbers working with

89

him? Is he into robbery?

MRS COLE: How could you think like that? You know we have enough wealth that can last our generation to another.

MRS DANIEL: That's what makes me wonder. *(Outside the house, Rosita drives into Chief Daniel's premises with Martins sitting beside her. The car is parked away from the maim entrance.)*

ROSITA: ...Augustine's parents must have come to appeal to my parents to get him out of the hook. My father talked on the phone as if he doesn't know you. So you need to pretend too.

MARTINS: Okay. I understand.

ROSITA: I will go inside first and act the way he expects me to behave. I'll call you on the phone to join us later.

MARTINS: All right. *(Rosita gets down from the car and goes into the house.)*

CHIEF DANIEL: I have to get to the bottom of this... *(Rosita opens the door and comes in. He stands up suddenly when she enters.)* Rosita, what the hell is going since we've gone to Abuja?

ROSITA: *(goes to lean against the wall, looking briefly at everyone in the sitting room.)* Like I've always been telling you, Augustine is a very violent man.

CHIEF DANIEL: You leave that to us to judge and tell me what I want to know.

ROSITA: I told you I cannot marry Augustine. So I took the advantage of your absence to marry the man I actually love.

CHIEF DANIEL: You're telling me you are truly married?

ROSITA: *(silently.)* Yes.

CHIEF DANIEL: Okay, we'll get back to that later. Tell me how come Augustine is arrested for the robbery in the house of the man you married?

ROSITA: *(looks down at her feet as every eye is on her.)* Augustine got to know about the marriage and hired men to kill my husband. The first attempt was made when we were coming from a store. A car almost ran him down. The second attempt was made in his house on the pretense that it was a robbery. My husband was shot on the chest but the bullet was stopped from getting into his heart by the small Bible in his breast pocket. The hired killers thought they have killed him. They were eventually caught. When they were tortured, they confessed that Augustine sent them to get rid him. Augustine was arrested. He would have used his connection to go away with it if my husband did not use his position as a senior civil servant to stop him. *(She looks at Chief Daniel who looks at Dr*

Cole with surprise.)

CHIEF DANIEL: This is quite different from what you told us. Do you have any reasons for the difference in the stories?

DR COLE: We are only saying what Augustine told us. We wouldn't know if he's telling the truth or not.

CHIEF DANIEL: My wife asked a moment ago what linked the robbery to Augustine. You said it was because the men worked for him. Do you mean to tell me you are not aware of this side of the story?

DR COLE: *(silently.)* No, actually.

ROSITA: With due respect, I don't believe you.

CHIEF DANIEL: *(There is silence as he sighs.)* Can you tell me what exactly you want me to do now?

MRS COLE: Augustine is languishing in the cell now. We want you to help us get him out.

CHIEF DANIEL: *(spreads his hands in a gesture.)* How am I supposed to do that? I'm not the one who arrested him.

DR COLE: We've talked to those in charge of the case. They said the only way our son can get out of the problem is to appeal to Rosita's husband.

CHIEF DANIEL: You talk as if I know this man. You think it's easy for me to think of my only daughter getting married to the man I don't know, let alone asking him for a favour?

DR COLE: Considering the situation, I have to beg you for the favour.

CHIEF DANIEL: If there is anybody to ask for that favour, it is Rosita; not me.

MRS DANIEL: We've asked her several times. She refused. We were hoping that when you come, you can appeal to her.

ROSITA: The law must take its course. *(She looks at Mrs Daniel.)* The question I asked you is that: what would have happened if Augustine had succeeded with his plan? I would become a widow.

CHIEF DANIEL: By the way, you are supposed to come with the man.

ROSITA: He's around.

MRS COLE: *(quickly responses.)* Can we appeal to him, please?

ROSITA: There is no use. As long as Augustine is a free man, his life is not save.

DR COLE: We promise you nothing will happen to him. In fact, we'll do whatever you want us to do to show that we not only release you to the man you have married but also wish you well. We can even sigh an undertaking if you want us to do that. All we want is the release of Augustine. By now he has learnt his bitter lesson form the problem.

Already, my name is in the mud. I wish I know how to redeem my reputation.

CHIEF DANIEL: *(looks at Rosita before going to sit down.)* Do whatever they want you to do.

ROSITA: If they can give me the assurance that Augustine will leave us alone in peace, then we'll get him out.

MRS DANIEL: You talk as if you can speak for him.

ROSITA: He is my husband. *(She takes her phone to call Martins.)* I can speak for him because he's a man I can predict… Hello, Martins. You can come and join us now. *(There is a brief silence before Martins opens the door and comes in.)* Martins, these are my parents…

CHIEF DANIEL: Forget about the introduction for now. Do what you are told to do.

ROSITA: *(shrugs and waves at Dr and Mrs Cole.)* I'm sure you know them.

MARTINS: Yes.

ROSITA: They have assured us that Augustine will leave us alone. So let the guy go.

MARTINS: *(looks at Chief Daniel and Mrs Daniel.)* If that's what you have decided, okay.

DR COLE: *(responses at once.)* Can we see the police inspector right away?

MARTINS: There's no need. I'll call to let him know my decision.

DR COLE: *(stands up to shake Martins' hand.)* Thank you very much. *(He looks at Chief Daniel.)* Thank you very much, Chief. *(Mrs Cole stands up.)* We'll see you later. *(They make for the door.)*

CHIEF DANIEL: Tell Augustine how much he disappointed me and advise him against hooliganism. It can cost him his life.

DR COLE: With the way he was brutalized by the police, I'm sure he has learnt his lesson. I will still te him anyway. *(They leave the room and go into their car outside and then drive away.)*

CHIEF DANIEL: You may not understand how hard it is for us to pretend that we didn't know anything about the wedding. *(He stands up.)* I have to congratulate you that you fought and won the battle with Augustine. I didn't know he is mean enough to take the battle this far. *(He stretches out his hand at Martins who quickly goes to take it. Chief Daniels draws him close and embraces him. Mrs Daniel opens her arm for Rosita who quickly goes to hug her.)*

MRS DANIEL: Congratulations for finding a man you can love and predict.

PLAY THREE

MASTER OF DISASTER

(Story Of The Spirit Eyes Series)

ACT ONE SCENE ONE

(Mama Seyi and Biodun are in the sitting room, chatting.)

MAMA SEYI: … Isn't God wonderful? He ensures that he meets our needs. He blesses us so much that we have no reason to complain.

BIODUN: Mum, so many families are suffering. Does that mean God loves us more than the rest?

MAMA SEYI: Oh, no my dear. God is not partial at all. The truth is: once we obey God in all will do, we'll have no problem at all.

BIODUN: That means many people who are suffering don't always obey God.

MAMA SEYI: Well… em it may not be but the usual course of problems is disobedience to the word of God. *(Seyi comes in to the sitting room, bouncing his ball.)* Seyi, how many times am I supposed to tell you not to play ball in the sitting room?

SEYI: *(stops bouncing the ball.)* Sorry, mum. *(He goes to sit down.)* Is the food ready? I'm so hungry that I'm ready to eat anything I see.

MAMA SEYI: You can eat your ball.

SEYI: Oh, mum…

MAMA SEYI: Are we your servants that will do the cooking while you play around?

SEYI: Boys play ball while mummies and the girls cook in the kitchen.

BIODUN: Let the boys eat the ball!

SEYI: Shut up your mouth. I'm not taking to you.

MAMA SEYI: She is right. You go and eat your ball. There is no food for you.

SEYI: Oh, mum, please! *(Just then, Baba Seyi opens the front door and comes inside the sitting room. The children quickly go to welcome him.)*

BIODUN: Welcome, dad. *(She takes the brief case in his hand, kneeling.)*

SEYI: *(bows.)* Welcome, sir.

BABA SEYI: *(looks happy.)* Hello, everybody. *(He goes to plant a kiss on Mama Seyi's cheek)*

MAMA SEYI: *(smiles.)* Welcome. *(She looks at Seyi and Biodun.)* The two of you can go see what we're cooking in the kitchen. *(The children leave for the kitchen. She stares at Baba Seyi who goes to sit beside her.)* I'm sure you have some good news to share with me.

BABA SEYI: (pretends to look serious.) I wonder what makes you think I've got any good news for you.

MAMA SEYI: *(smiles at him.)* You don't know how to hide both good and bad news. *(There is silence.)* I running out of patience. So tell me now.

BABA SEYI: Guess what, you're right! I've won the big contract that would earn us about twenty million!

MAMA SEYI: (screams.) Praise God! *(The children run out of the kitchen to join them.)*

SEYI: What's it, mum?

BABA SEYI: Oh, she's just excited that I won a big contract.

BIODUN: *(looks excited as well as Seyi.)* Wonderful!

SEYI: God is really great. We can get anything we want now, can't we, dad?

BABA SEYI: Oh, yes!

BIODUN: How about those who are in need? We must not forget them. That's what God says.

BABA SEYI: Oh, you and your mother are just the same. God will take care of them as he's taking care of us.

MAMA SEYI: We'll still need to sow into their lives. God tells us to always remember the needy when he blesses us.

BABA SEYI: Once we pay our tithes, I think that's okay.

MAMA SEYI: We really have to do more than that. God says he who much is given, much is required. We're talking about twenty million here.

SEYI: Twenty what?

BABA SEYI: You heard her right. Twenty million naira!

BIODUN: We don't need that kind of money!

BABA SEYI: Oh yes, we do. By the time we start buying things like fine cars - build houses and things like that, you will see that we'll need more...

ACT ONE SCENE TWO

(The Lord is on the throne when Red Spirit appears before him, roaring with anger.)

RED SPIRIT: *(bows before the Lord.)* Lord, Lord!

THE LORD: what are you looking for, disaster spirit?

RED SPIRIT: I've come here with the case of the family you established on the earth.

THE LORD: Do you have any problem with the family?

RED SPIRIT: I have complaints about everybody in that family. The couple are serving you because you bless them with money and children. If you give me permission to take away their money, you'll see that they'll deny you!

THE LORD: They'll not deny me. At least, not all of them will.

RED SPIRIT: Let me go and deal with them. We'll see the one that'll deny you.

THE LORD: All right. I give you the permission.

RED SPIRIT: If anyone deny you, can I take at least one life in family?

THE LORD: I give you the permission.

RED SPIRIT: *(jumps up it joy.)* Phew! Wonderful! I'm going to have some fun!*(He disappears.)*

ACT ONE SCENE THREE

(Mama Seyi, Seyi and Biodun are watching the television as Baba Seyi comes into the sitting room, looking very sorrowful. They look and greet him in different ways.)

MAMA SEYI: You look sad. What's wrong?

BABA SEYI: *(gives her a document and sits down.)* Can you believe that the minister of works and housing has the guts to tell me that the contract was meant for me?

MAMA SEYI: *(frowns as she reads the letter.)* What?!

BABA SEYI: The contract was taken away from me and awarded to anther contractor.

MAMA SEYI: *(looks stunned.)* Oh, my God! They can't do that, not after investing everything we have in the contract!

BABA SEYI: The minister just ruined us. The most painful aspect of this mess is that we're now neck deep with debts. The bank would eject us out of this house if I don't pay the loan I obtain from her. I wonder why God did this to us! We serve him with everything we have. We did all we could to please him yet he did this to us!

MAMA SEYI: I'm sure God didn't do this. The devil must have done it.

BABA SEYI: You mean to say the devil is more powerful?

MAMA SEYI: God must have permitted him.

BABA SEYI: *(looks angry.)* God permitted him? Why should he permit a thing like that?

MAMA SEYI: I may not be able to explain why but I know there is always a purpose for everything the Lord does.

BABA SEYI: The purpose cannot justify the consequences of this mess. So if the devil did it, then let me go and appeal to him to give back the contract before we are doomed!

97

MAMA SEYI: You can't do that! You can't turn to the devil because he took something from you.

BABA SEYI: Why not? If appealing to him can get it back, ...

MAMA SEYI: *(cuts in.)* You can't take anything from the devil without expecting him to take something from you.

BABA SEYI: We serve God and we lost everything in a single day! Surely, if the devil has anything to take from us, it can't be as much as what we have lost.

MAMA SEYI: We've not lost much. At least, we've not lost any member of our family. And we still have hope and peace.

BABA SEYI: Listen to yourself! With what has happened so far, you still believe we have peace? Perhaps you want us to wait until we are thrown into the street without a roof before you understand we've lost everything, including hope - and what you call peace!

MAMA SEYI: *(shakes her head regretfully)* I don't believe you're going to serve the devil because of money.

BABA SEYI: I never say I'll serve the devil, did I? All I want from him is the contract he took from me. I'll give him whatever he wants. Surely, he can't ask for more than goats or chicken. If I give it him, it's called negotiation. After all, you're the one that said it's him that took the contract. And the bible says, "give unto Caesar what is Caesar's." In other words, we can give to the devil what belongs to him and he'll give to us what belongs to us!

MAMA SEYI: Negotiating with the devil and serving him is the same thing, no matter the way you look at it!

BABA SEYI: If that's the way you see it, fine! I'll negotiate or serve him if God who is supposed to stop him from getting us into this mess is the one that allows him to take away everything we have in the family!

MAMA SEYI: No! *(Baba Seyi stands up to go out.)* Where are going you now?

BABA SEYI: I'm going to a witch doctor.

MAMA SEYI: I say no!

BABA SEYI: Are you giving me orders? Has it come to that? See what I mean when I say there is peace again. Now listen: as from now on, none of you will go to the church until I get the contract the devil takes from me.

MAMA SEYI: You can't stop me from going to the church.

BABA SEYI: You try me and see what happens! *(He rushes out of the sitting room angrily. Mama Seyi looks confused as she hurries out of the house as well.)*

98

ACT ONE SCENE FOUR

(Pastor is in the Church leaning backward on one of the pews. He seems asleep. The Lord suddenly appears in the Church in front of him, sitting on a golden chair. The red spirit appears before him, looking happy.)

RED SPIRIT: *(bows before the Lord.)* My Lord, I told you the man would deny you. I only took his money and he has already denied you.

THE LORD: His wife and children never deny me.

RED SPIRIT: Give me permission to take one life in the family, you'll see that the rest will deny you.

THE LORD: You can take it if the man in question does not come back to me. If he comes back, touch no one and give back all you've taken from the family.

RED SPIRIT: He wont come back to you. He's gone to one of my servants who will initiate him into my fold. *(He bows again and leaves. The Lord looks thoughtful.)*

THE LORD: I'm about to lose souls unless somebody do something about this. *(He disappears. Just then Mama Seyi bursts into the Church, panting heavily. Pastor wakes up with a start.)*

MAMA SEYI: Pastor! Pastor! There is trouble! *(He turns to look at her as if he is trying to wake up into reality.)* I'm so sorry to wake you up. We're so troubled in my family that I've been going from one place to another, looking for you. I've been to your house. I ....

PASTOR: *(looks a little awake, robbing his face with his palm.)* Madam... calm down.

MAMA SEYI: *(takes a deep breath.)* Okay, sir.

PASTOR: The Lord was giving me e revelation when you came. I don't know if it has anything to do with your family.

MAMA SEYI: *(without hesitation.)* Tell me about it.

PASTOR: Well, the Lord appears in that place. *(He points to the place.)* A red spirit appears in front of him with a report about a family that was blessed by the Lord. He said he just took the money he gave to the family and the man have already denied the Lord. *(Mama Seyi makes face.)* The spirit said that the man cannot go back to the Lord because he has gone to his servant who will initiate him into the fold....

MAMA SEYI: *(looks stunned.)* Pastor, it's my family! I came to tell you that my husband has gone to a witch doctor to get back the contract he just lost! And... and to request you to talk to him!

99

PASTOR: *(looks concerned.)* In that case, your family needs serious prayers. The consequence of his action can give the devil the chance to wreck your family.

MAMA SEYI: Aaah! *(She goes on her kneels.)* Pastor, please, help me. You have to do something before the devil destroys my family. You know how much I love them.

PASTOR: I'll mobilize the prayer group to seriously intercede for your family. Meanwhile, I'll need to talk to your husband. With prayers, God can make him listen to me.

ACT ONE SCENE FIVE

(Seyi and Biodun are in the sitting room, looking unhappy.)

SEYI: I heard Mum and Dad arguing about God taking our money. Why do you think God took our money?

BIODUN: God did not take our money. The devil did. Besides, we don't have anything we can call our own. God gives and if he wants to take it, he has the right to take it.

SEYI: You make God appears like a bully to me. This is one of the reasons it's hard to serve God.

BIODUN: God is not a bully. We all know that. He is a loving and merciful God. If not, he would have destroyed this world that is full of sins and evils.

SEYI: If he is so loving and merciful, how do you explain what's happening to us now? We have money before now. See.... see... we've got nothing. From what Dad said, we'll soon become homeless.

BIODUN: God will not allow that to happen before he rescues us. You'll see.

SEYI: You trust God that much?

BIOUDUN: Yes!*(There's a knock on the door Biodun goes to open the door. Pastor comes in.)*

BIODUN: *(kneels before him.)* You're welcome, sir.

PASTOR: How are you, my dear.

BIODUN: We are fine.

SEYI: *(looks at her with contempt.)* What's fine in our condition..? Welcome, sir. Pastor, We are not fine at all!

PASTOR: *(smiles at him and goes to pat him on the shoulder.)* Seyi… There are some things you don't understand about life but if you study the Bible often you will understand many things. While coming, I overheard you saying God is a bully. I'm surprised that it's your sister that was teaching you what you are supposed

100

to teach her. As she was trying to tell you, God is not responsible for any of the evils around us. The devil is. The God we serve is good.

SEYI: I wish I can believe you, sir.

PASTOR: When God restores the blessing in your family, you will believe me then, wont you?

SEYI: Yes, I will. Until then, I wont.

PASTOR: I wish you don't act like Thomas who doubted the resurrection of Jesus Christ until he saw him. *(He looks at Biodun who is silent.)* Where are our parents?

BIODUN: They are in the room.

PASTOR: Tell them I'm around. *(He goes to take his seat while Seyi stands up to go to his room.)* I want you to be around as I share a few things with your parents .

SEYI: I'm sorry I cannot spare the time to listen. I need to read.

PASTOR: It wont take much time.

SEYI: *(shrugs and goes to sit down again.)* Okay. *(Biodun returns with her parents.)*

BABA SEYI: *(smiles slyly at Pastor .)* Pastor, how do you do.

PASTOR: *(smiles and stands up to shake hands with him.)* Good afternoon, sir. *(He looks at Mama Seyi who looks very gloomy.)* It's going to be well, Madam.

BABA SEYI: *(glances at him.)* Who told you things are not well?

PASTOR: The Lord reveal to me what is going on here.

BABA SEYI: Pastor, don't tell me that because I wont believe it.

MAMA SEYI: *(interrupts him.)* Please, sit down, sir. *(Pastor sits. The rest also sit on the chairs.)* What can I offer you?

PASTOR: Oh, no. I just took a heavy lunch before coming here.

MAMA SEYI: How about some drinks?

PASTOR: No. Thank you, ma. *(He looks at Baba Seyi.)* You doubt if God reveals anything to me.

BABA SEYI: I know so about the gimmicks which you guys who call yourselves men of God normally employ to get people to listen to you or do what you want.

MAMA SEYI: You are talking to the Pastor?

BABA SEYI: *(in a harsh voice.)* No, I don't know I'm talking to the Pastor, foolish woman!

PASTOR: It's okay, madam. Sometimes situation make us act differently. So let's not blame anyone for anything. *(He looks at Baba Seyi.)* God actually revealed to me what the family was going through until she came to me.

101

BABA SEYI: She came to you? *(Pastor nods.)* I see...

PASTOR: I've not come here to manipulate you.

BABA SEYI: Did I say that?

PASTOR: You don't have to say it before I read it on your face. Anyway, it was revealed to me that the devil was reporting this family to the Lord.

BABA SEYI: *(roars with angry laughter and stops suddenly, looking very irritated.)* What did the devil say I did to him before taking away everything I have?

PASTOR: That's what he does. He causes problems where there is peace, creates sorrow where there is joy and plants hatred where this love. God allows him at times to try our faith. If you can persevere and hope in the Lord, God will lift you up again. It's like the case of Job who went through so much problems and pains.

BABA SEYI: Listen to me, Pastor. I'm aware that you we're trained to do what you're doing now - give people hope. I appreciate that, honestly. However, you must understand that I will not waste my time serving the Lord or any other god that cannot deliver me. You're familiar with the adage that says that the god that cannot deliver me should leave me as he finds me. I was comfortable before knowing that Lord. I serve him but - see what happens. We don't have anything now except huge debts. *(He stands up to go.)*

PASTOR: Wait... *(Baba Seyi ignores him and leaves. He signs, looking at Mama Seyi who looks sadder.)* We'll pray that God should open his eyes to see what is happening. I hope it'll not be too late then. *(He stands up.)* It is well....

ACT TWO SCENE ONE

(Two weeks later. Seyi is in the sitting room, shivering. Mama Seyi and Biodun sit beside him. Both look dejected.)

MAMA SEYI: Oh, my Lord, what else are we supposed to do now? We've been to the hospital. The doctor said they could find anything wrong with you. Is this…. another trial or what?

BIODUN: Whatever it is, we'll not give up. When the Pastor comes, we'll take him to the Church for prayers.

MAMA SEYI: I hope he'll come before your father comes. He said he was going to one herbalist to get some drugs when he was going out.

BIODUN: Let's get him out of here before he comes back. *(As they attempt to lift him up, Baba Seyi bursts inside the room ,* *holding something that is wrapped in a paper.)*

BABA SEYI: I've brought some drugs. *(He unwraps the paper and reveals some black powder inside.)*

BIODUN: *(grumbles impatiently.)* Dad, we can't allow you to give him the item you got from the devil.

BABA SEYI: *(looks surprised.)* What did you say? *(There is silence.)* I don't have time for you yet. *(He gestures her to get up from Seyi's side while he takes her place.)*

MAMA SEYI: *(holds his hand as he attempts to take some of the powder.)* Baba Seyi, as Biodun said, we can't allow you to give this medicine to the boy.

BABA SEYI: *(in angry voice.)* What is your problem, woman?

MAMA SEYI: You're the problem! You're the one doing things your own way. You have no respects for our opinions.

BABA SEYI: We've tried the hospital. It failed. What else do you want us to do? Wait for nothing to happen?

MAMA SEYI: Let's take him to the Church.

BABA SEYI: When did the pastor turn into a doctor? Look here, woman. If you try to get on my nerves once again, I will squeeze life out of you!

MAMA SEYI: Let's ask the boy if he wants what you're about to give to him. We can resolve the matter that way. *(She looks at Seyi.)* Seyi, you have to decide if you want your father to give you the black powder he got from a witch doctor or not. *(The rest look at Seyi. He moans and nods.)* What does that mean?

BABA SEYI: He says he wants the medicine.

MAMA SEYI: *(still looking at Seyi.)* You want the medicine? *(Seyi nods again. She and Biodun look disappointed.)* Well, the choice is yours.

BABA SEYI: *(looks glad.)* That's my boy. *(He takes some of the powder.)* Open your mouth and lick this. *(Seyi opens his mouth slowly and licks the powder.)* Good boy. *(A moment later, Seyi begins to moan, holding his stomach. Biodun and Mama Seyi look agitated.)* The doctor said he'll have slight pain. *(Seyi becomes tensed with pain until his body eventually becomes lifeless.)*

MAMA SEYI: *(frantically examines Seyi.)* Oh, Lord! Seyi... He's not breathing! *(She begins to scream, pulling Baba Seyi's cloth.)* What have you done to him!

ACT TWO SCENE TWO

(After another week, Mama Seyi sits with Biodun. Both look sorrowful. The door is knocked. Biodun goes to open it.)

PASTOR: *(comes inside.)* Hello, Biodun.

BIODUN: *(kneels down.)* Welcome, Sir.

MAMA SEYI: *(stands up from the couch.)* Pastor, you've come to see us again?

PASTOR: *(in a quiet voice.)* Yes. I have to. This is the time the family needs the church most.

MAMA SEYI: You can have your seat, sir.

PASTOR: *(goes to take a seat.)* Where is your husband?

MAMA SEYI: The lunatic is in the room. He dare not come near where I am.

PASTOR: You have to forgive him. I keep telling you this.

MAMA SEYI: It's hard to forgive him. *(She begins to sob.)* We have only two child but we're happy until he killed one.

PASTOR: God will give you another one.

MAMA SEYI: God will give us a son that is as old as Seyi?

PASTOR: Please, learn to do away with the past. It can prevent you from moving on with your life.

MAMASEYI: *(shrugs.)* Okay. *(Pastor brings out envelop and hands it to her.)*

PASTOR: This is from the church.

MAMA SEYI: *(in whispers.)* I'm so grateful. I don't know how we could have survived all we've gone through in the past few weeks without the church.

PASTOR: We're members of the same body of Christ, remember. If one suffers, the rest feel the pains too. *(He stands up.)* I have to go now. I'll see you again.

MAMA SEYI: Thank you so much, sir.... *(She also stands up.)*

ACT TWO SCENE THREE

(At night, Baba Seyi sleeps in the room when the Lord appears, sitting on the chair. The red spirit appears before him, roaring with laughter.)

THE LORD: What do you want again, disaster spirit?

RED SPIRIT: I want to take the life of the father of the boy since he's the one denies you.

THE LORD: You requested to take only one life in the family if anyone of them denies me. I allowed you take the life of the boy because the father denied me by coming to you when he has problems.

RED SPIRIT: That's true. But you have to remember your word that says that the soul that sins shall die. Let me kill the one that denies you so that I can take him to hell.

THE LORD: *(looks thoughtful.)* I'm bound by my word. So if he does not repent, you can do whatever you like to him.

RED SPIRIT: Thank you, my Lord!*(He disappears.)*

THE LORD: *(shakes his head sadly.)* My people perish for lack of knowledge. *(He disappears. After a while Baba Seyi wakes up with a start, screaming on top of his voices.)*

BABA SEYI: (r*uns round frantically in the room.)* Mama Seyi ooo! Biodun! *(He looks confused.)* Where are they? They must have gone to the Church. I must go and meet them there! I don't want to die! devil, get thee behind me! *(He runs out of the house.)*

ACT TWO SCENE FOUR

(The Pastor is leading the rest in prayers with everybody including Mama Seyi and Biodun praying fervently. Then Baba Seyi bursts into the Church, looking nervous.)

BABA SEYI: *(on top of his voice.)* I am dead ooo! *(He goes to pull the Pastor's legs as everybody looks startled.)* Pastor, the devil will kill me unless you help me!

PASTOR: What happened?

BABA SEYI: *(pants heavily.)* I saw the devil in a dream! He said he wants to kill me because I denied the Lord! *(There is long silence as moans with deep regrets.)*

PASTOR: *(smiles as others looks amused. He pulls him up on his feet.)* I thank God that He opened your eyes to the truth at last. Well, since you have run back to the Lord, He will never cast you away. But I want you to learn a valuable lesson here. No matter what we are passing through, you must not give up your faith in the Lord. As you can see that so much depends on our faith in the Lord. If you have stuck to Him, your son would still be alive. As the saying goes, a word is enough for the wise. So let's pray.... *(He begins to lead the rest in prayer.)*

responsible parents also learnt wrong things from them. He decided to follow his father's footsteps by taking alcohol when he was in primary school. As if that was not bad enough, he tried to teach other children in the school the madness in his home. A school teacher, however, was able to influence him and his mother by teaching them Christian morals. Even then, Junior was soon caught in the crossfire at home as his father tried to enlist him as a future member of a secret cult that posed as a social club.

SUCCESSFUL CHRISTIANITY AND BASIC MINISTRIES
ISBN: 978-49874-6-0
A Collection Of Resource Materials That Precedes Christian Ministries And Basic Leadership Course Book

The first question is how Christianity is practiced even in a hostile environment. Next to that is the question about the potentials of Christians in spite of their apparent limitations. The other issues are connected to the successes, deliverance, callings, basic ministries of all Christians and evangelism. Various schools of thoughts have attempted these questions but many answers only portray Christianity as a form of religion instead of a way of life as specified by God. Some answers give room for compromise, hypocrisies, dogmas and denominational doctrines. The misconceptions about these areas of Christianity have brought about worldliness instead of righteousness and false achievements instead of fulfillment.

This book which contains six different subjects had been used to hold seminars at various levels, train ministers and Christian workers in Bible Schools and to equip the Church. It explains in simple terms the seemingly complex issues on practice of Christianity, Potentials, Deliverance, God's Kind Of Success, Evangelism and Basic Ministries of a Christian with Biblical principles, life transforming stories and illustrations.

INSANITY OF HUMANITY
ISBN: 978-36348-6-0 ISBN: 978-978-36348-6-2
The Results Of Research Works Into Various Methods Of Brainwashing

Man is made to exercise his freewill. The mind of his own and the power to choose between right and wrong, good and evil, light and darkness is about to be washed away through brainwashing. The agents of control dubbed as Secret Government by John Todd (the top Illuninati defector) have put necessary machinery in place to ensure that all human beings are in conformity in their thinking and ways of life, trying to wipe away diversity, which makes each person unique.

This book attempts to shed light on how the techniques of mind control are applied through the use of propaganda, education, entertainments, drugs, religions, media and other means of communications. It is the result of research works, some of which are based on findings of various researchers and writers like Bugger Lugz, Edward Hunter, Hadley Cantril, Herbert Krugman, David L. Robb, Vaughan Bell, Juliana Gomez, Ryan Duffy Vice, Henry Makow, David Nicholls, Fritz Springmeire, Steven Hassan, Renate Thienel, Debra Pursell, Mary Pride and a host of others who are acknowledged in this book.

NO MORE TEARS TO SHED
ISBN: 978-49874-3-0 ISBN: 978-978-74-3-1

Kidnappers took Tokunbo away from his grand parents in a city in Nigeria when he was a little boy. A nice woman found him in another town and gave him a false identity. She spoilt him with love, making him to grow into a rebellious teenager that was not appreciated anywhere. When Janet made him a Christian, however, life began to make sense to him until the day he was beaten to the point of death for the offence he knew nothing about. He left the town for the city which, unknown to him, held his true identity and the link to his parents in the United States. To find them was only a question of time.

THE UNROMANTIC LOVE BIRDS
ISBN: 978-4987-5-7 ISBN: 978-978-4974-5-5
And other short stories about love and marriages

They were very much in love right from their school days but when they got married and had children, romance became the game Charles' wife refused to play. No matter how much he tried to make her understand the unbearable condition her unromantic attitude has subjected him into, she would not change. Consequently, after enduring for so long, he was forced to look for the women that would make up for her weakness. He unofficially married a beautiful lady of insane jealousy. Though she was ready to give him

what was missing in his marriage, it soon dawn on him that he has solved one big problem only to create a bigger one.

THE BATTLE OF THE CONQUERORS
ISBN: 978-49874-7-3 ISBN: ISBN: 978-978-49874-0-7-9
Wickedness takes over the land of Bondage from First Couple and subjects everybody into slavery without giving anybody the chance to

be free. Love brings The Redeemer from Eternity and offers the slaves the chance to escape. Wickedness soon declares war and engages everyone in the battle. The Redeemer makes the redeemed people Conquerors by giving them the armour of war and Comforter but Wickedness cannot be undone. He has several thousands of years of experience in the war. So he is quick to recognize the weakness of the redeemed people who are ignorant of their strengths and advantages. Although the Conquerors fight like immutable giants, rescuing victims of war, many people suffer heavy casualties.

Since King Wickedness knows that a redeemed person is strong enough to chase one thousand of his warriors at a time, and two would put ten thousand into flight, he enlists as one of his warriors the people's deadliest enemy called Disunity.

Wickedness is able to strike the people by making them to fight with one another, turning what is supposed to be their best moments in the battle into tales of woes.

BLOODSHED IN CAMPUS
ISBN: 978-07350-3-8 ISBN: 978-978-07350-3-6

A poor widow tearfully warned her son, Richard, against joining the bad wagon when he got an admission into one of the Nigerian Universities. He resisted the membership of groups of students, including the Christian Fellowship until he had an encounter with a member of The Black Skulls - a deadly and ruthless secret cult on the campus.

Before Richard knew what he was up against, the head of The Black Skulls had arranged items for his initiation into the cult. While resisting being initiated, he ran to the Christian Fellowship for help. The leader of the Christian Fellowship dragged The President of Students' Union Government (S.U.G) into the conflict. With the involvement of the S.U.G President, another formidable cult called The Red Eyes felt obliged to team up against The Black Skulls. Then the campus turned into a battlefield and BLOODSHED became the order of the black day.

NETWORK BIBLE CLUB
YOUTH AND ADULT BOOK ONE
ISBN: 978 - 978- 49874-9-X ISBN: 978-978-49874-9-3
A collection of 26 life transforming stories, 26 poems, 26 hymn tuned songs and weekly Bible lessons

The issue of moral instructions in schools and at homes is threatened with extinction. Consequently, so many youths are involved in prostitution, drug addictions, cultism, fraudulent practices, armed robberies and other crimes. Those who are supposed to be trained as leaders in various walks of life are the ones posing serious threats to many lives. Many parents who fail to add moral values to the upbringing of their children often times breed potential criminals under their roofs without knowing it. Apart from these, many other people negatively influence young ones through the media, music, publications, films, conduct and foul language; making them to lose their moral and family values.

This book one just like the rest of other volumes is an attempt to bring back moral instructions into schools and campuses through the use of stories, hymn tuned songs, poems, Bible lessons and class activities. It is designed to assist teachers and ministers in Secondary Schools, Bible Clubs, Churches and Campus Fellowships to teach people, especially youths the Word of God and serves as a school text book in subjects relating to literature, music and other creative works.

FOUNDATION BIBLE CLUB A-Z STORY BOOK
ISBN: 978-49874-2-2 ISBN: 978-978-49874-2-4
Volume 1 With 26 Stories, 26 Bible
Lessons, 26 Rhymes And 26 Songs For Book For Young Minds

An adage says, "a man who builds a house without building his child builds what the child will later sell." Proverbs 22:6 says, "train up a child in the way he should go: and when he is old, he will not depart from it." This book is an attempt to assist parents and teachers to meet up to the challenges that befall them in carrying out this important function in the light of the moral decadence that is prevailing all over the world.

The first edition of the book was used by several thousands of teachers, ministers and parents in schools, Churches and homes to build the moral values of young ones. Apart from the stories, songs and Bible passages for the young ones to study, there is a seminar material that is based on the lecture which the author delivered to school proprietors, children ministers and Christian professionals in this volume.

THE WEIGHT OF DEATH
ISBN: 9978-36348-0-1 ISBN: 978-978-36348-0-0
(Story Of The Spirit Eyes Series)

PLAY ONE: HORROR IN THE FAMILY: Talimi probably did not envisage his death when he was trying to compel his son, Damola to succeed him in the occult Brotherhood. Other members of the secret cult were aware of the battle between them. So when Talimi died; his family, especially Damola who was a diehard Christian began to fall prey to the cult. Using all their powers and the spirit that posed as Talimi's ghost, the cult waged war against the family, tormenting and making them to be at loggerheads.

PLAY TWO: RITUAL KIDS' KIDNAPPERS: Victor and the rest of the members of the School Bible Club were taught that there are lots of evil people in this world but he did not understand why God allowed him to be among the children that were taken away from their parents. He soon understood that he was to be used by God to rescue other children who did not know that everyone that truly believes in Jesus has the power to overcome evil.

PLAY THREE: THE WEIGHT OF DEATH: Awoseun would not have known the real source of problems of mankind if his father had not given him the power to see demons tormenting the people in different ways. What he was yet to know, however, was the power of light over darkness. When he was caught in crossfire between these powers, he desperately sought for deliverance.

CALVARY ROCK RESOURCE BOOKLETS
ISSN: 1595 93X
The Quarterly Missionary Booklets That Are Designed To Teach Children, Youths And Adults In Schools, Fellowships, Churches, At Homes, Office And Other Places.

Although all the various volumes of this booklet can be used independently of other books but it is recommended that it should be used as part of supplementary materials to make up for Foundation and Network Bible Club Story Books for both children and adults in School, Church, Campus, Office and other Fellowships.

Each of the volume is rich with quarterly Bible lessons, stories, drama, songs, seminar, tract materials and a host of other things that can be used to edify, educate, entertains and evangelize every category of people, ranging from children to elderly persons.

Every volume is designed to equip school teachers, ministers in Churches or campus or office fellowships and other people who wish

to work with the Lord.